# ADVANCE PRAISE FOR PURE GOLD

'John Patrick McHugh's stories are full of stylish brio, headlong with energy, and pulse with real feeling and depth. He is a young writer forging a fresh and intense new path through the landscape of Irish letters.' COLIN BARRETT

'McHugh writes very tenderly about people, and very vibrantly about place. *Pure Gold* describes the dull lives of a splendid island, in prose that is always splendid and never dull.' SARA BAUME

'McHugh's stories are monoliths that glitter with piercing detail, sunlit with godlike purpose and control.' GAVIN CORBETT

'John Patrick McHugh is a wildly ambitious craftsman, and such a thrilling writer of sentences.' DANNY DENTON

'This is a terrific collection. The stories are dark, funny, honest and engrossing.' RODDY DOYLE

'I've long been an admirer of John Patrick McHugh's precise and focused fiction. I've eagerly awaited each new piece of work. I'm so excited that these insightful, emotionally intelligent and savagely funny stories will now reach a wider audience. *Pure Gold* is a striking literary debut.' NICOLE FLATTERY

'This collection is refreshing and ambitious, its stories full of heart and balls and mischief.' LISA McINERNEY

'This astonishing collection of stories draws the reader into a world at once familiar and deliciously strange – the world of a fictional island community off the coast of County Mayo. With an unflinching eye for injustice, cruelty and self-deceit, McHugh nonetheless approaches his cast of characters with a sincere and intelligent compassion. These stories bring to life not only the individual lives of human people, but the collective life of a whole community. In exquisite and arresting prose, this collection make it clear that John Patrick McHugh is one of the most exciting writers working in Ireland today.' SALLY ROONEY

JOHN PATRICK McHUGH

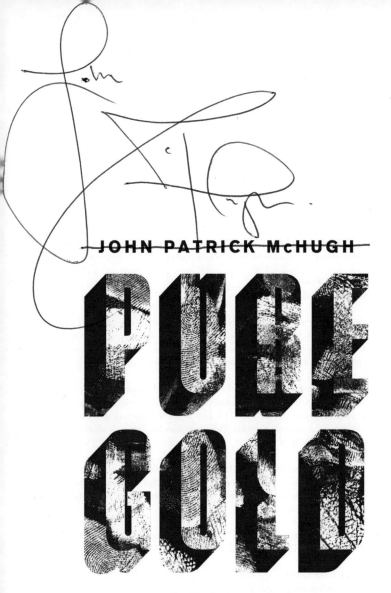

# PURE GOLD

*STORIES*

NEW ISLAND

PURE GOLD
First published in 2021 by
New Island Books
Glenshesk House
10 Richview Office Park
Clonskeagh
Dublin D14 V8C4
Republic of Ireland
www.newisland.ie

Print ISBN: 978-1-84840-791-6
eBook ISBN: 978-1-84840-792-3

'Bonfire' appeared in *Winter Papers*, volume 2, 2016; 'Pure Gold' appeared on granta.com, May 2016; 'Hoarfrost' appeared on granta.com, October 2018; 'Howya, Horse' appeared in *Banshee*, issue 10, autumn/winter 2020; 'The First Real Time' appeared in *The Stinging Fly*, issue 38, volume 2, summer 2018 and 'Bury It' appeared as 'Bury My Heart' in *The Tangerine*, issue 1, winter 2016.

British Library Cataloguing in Publication Data. A CIP catalogue record for this book is available from the British Library.

Typeset by JVR Creative India
Edited by Neil Burkey, neilburkey.com
Cover design by Jack Smyth, jacksmyth.co
Printed by L&C Printing Group, Poland

New Island received financial assistance from The Arts Council (An Chomhairle Ealaíon), Dublin, Ireland.

New Island Books is a member of Publishing Ireland.

*For Mam and Dad*

# CONTENTS

# Bonfire

That summer we lit fires. Terry and I.

We'd meet in the mornings, when oats still gummed my molars and the sky was beginning to shake itself blue. Two of us dressed in thready-sleeved jerseys; two of us decorated with scabs and cuts and small, sloughing burnholes. When we had money, we chucked it together and bought matches from Brett's Newsagent. And when we had no spare coppers – the more likely – we snatched clickety lighters from the dashboard of Terry's dad's van or bummed fizzing matches from the backyard smokers of The Clinic. Then, bodies gunned over the handlebars of our bikes, we'd thunder on in pursuit of fires, the Island quaking from our shouts. Time had no use to us. Days never had acts, never dulled to a yawn, never became sticky; rather they were endless, borderless, buzzing alive until we were confronted by the full stop of night.

There was no wind on the day of the bonfire. To the south, the sky's edge was brick-red and the clouds – mirrored in the puddles about the field – held this same rubyglow in their fleeces. Terry was on the ground, the canister clamped between his thighs. I was crouched beside him, acting like I wasn't paying much attention as he wrestled with the screwed-tight lid. But with each failed attempt, I noted how Terry's expression twisted; his eyes bunching to wrinkles, how the lighter fuel made this vexing plopping sound. All of a sudden, Terry yelled fury and brought the lid to his mouth, and using the girth of his teeth, slowly, slowly, slowly grinded it open. Blood trickled from his mouth as we poured the fuel over the plywood and tyres and branches and cardboard and pallets and paper and hay. Already the bonfire seemed to sizzle.

At first, we lit little ones. Teeny fires. Sparking the tips of grass, burning copybooks, comics, photos pried from under frames. We melted Action Man dolls, slugs, milk cartons, plastic bottles, and loved when they softened to wax and glop. Soon our fingertips hardened, became scaly, snake-skinned, and we dared ourselves to be braver. We burnt the bushy tail of Miss O'Donnell's cat, ravaged to crap a long shade of heather, and flicked a match into a bin down by Keel's caravan site, pinching our privates from behind a nearby wall as we watched a lanky fella scramble for a hose. Once we discovered Brendan Hare lurking near our field. Terry pinned him down and like a skilled craftsman, my teeth biting into my tongue, I singed the faint lace hair on his arms and brow. Hare, two years younger than us, cried for his mother, runners kicking into the earth, but we didn't stop. There was something in fire that we needed. And so, we hunted after the cocky spark and clank of the lighter, the peacock-ruffle of a catching blaze, the flame and all its bold promises.

We scoured the whole Island for the bonfire. Snapping branches from trees and hedges, stuffing hay from sheeted bales into plastic bags. We visited Dr Gaffney's newest extension, our knees grazed to chalk as we borrowed planks and prickly pallets. One drab night we even snuck into Flannery's Garage. Barely breathing, we nicked three tyres and a bundle of rubber cord.

I found a shed nestled in the east corner of the Pineneedle Woods. It was loaded with crusted spray cans and weedkiller. Hairy thistles creeped up from the floorboards along with bustling woodlice. We guessed an ancient forester's den. Terry declared it our base and we swore the shed's existence to deathly, eye-gouging, dick-snipping secrecy. We cleared everything out and, piece by crummy piece, stashed the bonfire inside. Thereafter our foraging became instinctive. If one of us was away, the other still trawled the Island with gamey hands, thieving anything that would burn. And when the evenings shortened and the wind began to stiffen and bully, we dragged the bonfire out to the field. Terry tackled the big stuff, the tyres and the planks; I carried the loose rotting wood and hay and the stacks of newspapers that I had spied unloved around the back of Sweeney's.

The field was tucked halfway between our houses. An uneven patch of buttercups, clovers and spongey mustard grass. From there, you could see the roofs of Keel, the school, the water, and the red beams of the bridge. And always you could hear the drone of cars cruising along the Glon. We did everything in the field. Built traps for the wolves we hoped stalked us, sharpened swords out of the handles of brooms, practised our wrestling finishers; mine the Steel Choker, Terry's the Hell-Bells Suplex. When it rained, which was often, we sat atop two paint buckets in our makeshift hut – a sheet of metal slantways against the neighbouring barbed-wire fence. Our arms folded or slashing at legs eaten by bugs as we gawped at our world being made momentarily unusable. That summer we caught only one beast, and even that was happened upon rather than ensnared in one of our traps. A twitching hare. Terry brought it to the hut, holding it by the hind leg like a stocking, and I slit apart its stomach with a whetted rock. I don't know what we expected to uncover or why we even conducted this post-mortem. But I do remember the Vaseline-glossed muscles and the pulpy dark blood that didn't resemble blood. I remember we prodded at its wormy guts with our fingers, tugged at its long, velvety ears till the skin tore. I remember that throughout the hare's panicked eyes leered out at us, and I jumped once thinking I saw one of the chestnut globes blink. Later, we burned the corpse and buried its cindered bones in the centre of our field, carefully marking a pyramid of stones over it.

My older brother Mark told me about bonfires, about the ones he and his pals had built. He said he cooked bonfires that burnt the fuckin clouds. He told me how to stage a proper bonfire and I wrote everything down as if fire, the very thing Terry and I had mastered, was impossible without these ingredients in this order. The next morning, I explained the entire process to Terry while we scouted about. Terry nodded and nodded again and said he liked the idea of burning the clouds.

I also learned knacker from my brother. Terry had been over – we had played the PlayStation while it vomited down outside – and after waving him off, my brother pushed me as I wandered back into the playroom. You're hanging around knackers now, he teased. You can't find yourself any normal friends. I reddened but ordered myself to ignore him. He nudged me again: Mammy wouldn't like that. Her precious playing with knackers. Thinking about it, Mark said with a smirk, he's probably the one who gave you nits. My brother and I hadn't fought since June, so I took him by surprise when I swung for him. He laughed at my first punches but when I clocked him in the balls he went vicious. He slapped me twice and tossed my body to the floor, placing his knee against my shoulder. Like a gear, he worked my arm backwards until it was bent, and I felt a surge of fluorescent pain. Only when I screamed did he let go. Stupid gimp, he said, wheezing. Your friend's a knacker. A filthy rotten knacker. I didn't know the word's meaning, but I was chilled by how it left his lips then, as if it was wrong, like fuck, like bastard, as if it was venom. My dad rushed in and pulled Mark off me. And rightaway, I tattled, a hand nursing my elbow. I emphasised the bad word used. My dad stood between us, repeated my claims and the word itself. With a hand on my shoulder, he then said maybe I should be a little more aware about who I tag along with. But that he didn't appreciate that sort of language in his house. Or violence, for that matter. My brother mumbled something, and my dad shouted, Watch your mouth. Mark trudged out, slamming the door, and my dad chased after, leaving me alone in the playroom. The word ringing in my ears.

The next day I called Terry a knacker. We were digging through a bin and I abruptly remembered, as if pinched behind my knee, the hole in Terry's sock and the wonder he held for my PlayStation and the word, and so I said it. Carefully, Terry wiped his hands clean on his shorts before hitting me hard across the face. I fell and he planted himself on my stomach, pummelled my arm until I wept, Mercy. He didn't get off then, just inclined his head to the side and told me to not call him that ever again. I agreed, promised, squealing for air, though I still felt the word cower under my tongue. He raised his fist once more and I flinched and he stepped off. In the days after, I had a panting wish to say it. While we worked, I would mouth the word behind his back, at night I'd dream of shouting it in front of an audience. Knacker. Filthy Knacker. Suddenly, I knew what he was and more importantly, where I stood above him. I never invited Terry over again that summer. Once, when he mentioned the PlayStation and the tommy-gun boss on Crash we hadn't beaten, I replied casually without a lick of shame: Don't you know you're banned from my house? Terry stared at me for a long time but didn't contest.

I first met Terry when I lived with my mam in an estate out near The Valley. The estate was cut into the backside of a disused football pitch and plotted with six dingy holiday homes. It was Auntie Joan's house and Mam kept apologising about the state of it, about us actually having to live there. On the day I met Terry, I had been smacking a ball for hours at the wall across from the house. A pebbledash wall, about six foot high and filled with what seemed to be emeralds. Terry passed by and then came back again and sat himself on the curb opposite. He said something, his knuckles smudged into his cheeks, but I didn't answer. When I could hammer free not a single emerald, I started to rage, sickened at the world for not being shaped the way I wanted it to be. I screamed the few curse words I possessed while Terry asked what was I trying to do. I answered without a glance back, What do you think? Knock the wall, Terry responded matter-of-factly. When I didn't reply, he rose and repeated, You want to knock the wall. He strolled off, returning a minute or so later, skitting and hugging this massive rock to his chest. He said, This is how you do it, and launched the rock at the wall. Dust swarmed, surrounded. I heard the emeralds fall like night rain on glass. I giggled and I followed him to get more rocks. I don't think we spoke again that day. We just flung rock after rock at the wall until I saw my mam on the front step, bald as if wearing a swim cap. Embarrassed by the cut of her, I said, I'll see you tomorrow. Terry called after my shadow, Yeah, see you tomorrow.

In May they shut Mam into the hospital, and I moved back in with my dad and brother. Almost immediately, Terry and I forgot the estate and our man-made tunnels and in a daze, began to find new schemes in the muddy trails spread between our houses. In the rare days we were sick of fires and the field, we'd walk through the bogs, barefooted, feeling the squelch of turf under our toes. Or on the few boiling afternoons, we'd explore the watery ditches between bank and road, not minding the crops of flies or the stings of the sunny gorse or the tepid smell of sewage. Our language was partial: 'Let's do this', 'Don't know', 'We go there'. Nothing outward mattered to us, we just chased something, real or dreamt, in the distance, following always the want to do things while the light was still good.

My dad worked in the bank in Westport and after the sixteenth of June, he must have decided that exhaustion was the most socially acceptable form of grief. He'd leave at eight in a dishevelled grey suit and return home at nine, his hair a little lifted from his forehead. He'd call me in for dinner – vinegary brown bags or something crumbed that could be placed in the oven – and sat with me as I ate.

We'd talk mainly about the football or chores he needed to do around the house or sometimes very vaguely about ourselves as if we were playing an especially lethargic round of Guess Who. Sometimes he'd complain about the dirt of my hands and the charcoal gunk on my shorts. He'd say her name then, as a sort of beacon that I could use to guide me. To remind me to stay out of trouble. For her sake at least, he'd say. I couldn't argue once her name was mentioned, as if he had forgotten their own rows or how she screamed terror at me and Mark. At the weekend, I'd find my dad scrubbing and hoovering the house like it was infected with lice, lightly scolding me that I should be helping him. I remember my eyes watering against the stench of polish from the living room, where my father was on his hands and knees with a yellow rag, buffing the border of the fireplace, the brass-tinted poker, the grill. Before him, spread out on the hemp rug, were the photographs from the mantelpiece: my communion photo, one of Mam, me and my brother, me and my brother with a parrot, their wedding day. The frames were already glistening, were already cleaned.

Terry won the right to light the bonfire. He nabbed the lighter fuel from under a neighbour's barbeque and so he earned the right. There was no jealousy on my part – we had worked hard for the bonfire and it was time for it to go. That was the way, we had to end our song. Terry's first match got a flash, but it vanished to a woof of smoke when he squatted down. The second didn't light at all.

I posed then as if it were nothing to me, but inside my heart drummed over the fear that we were going to run out of matches, that it would all be ruined, when in an instant Terry struck a match ice-blue. Shielding it with his left hand, he propped the matchhead against straw and a layer of cardboard. He turned to me, a big wide smile, his tongue peeking through the gap in his front teeth.

When Mam went into the hospital, my dad said she had leukaemia. My brother said she was fucked with cancer. I was brought to visit her every Wednesday and Friday. She was the only one in her room, hunched up in a bed with stern bars and levers, wearing a polka-dot headband that I had never seen before. She had no eyebrows and her face was like a rumpled sweet wrapper. Her new smile, narrow and picked with stitch-like indents, frightened me. I didn't want to touch her, even a glance disturbed. I stayed in the corner and waved hello, and a little later waved goodbye. After my first visit to the hospital, my father spent the drive home promising me all these marvellous, shiny things: the huge fish tank I didn't get for Christmas, the penknife she wouldn't allow, somehow he would expand my bedroom. At a red light, he twisted to look at me, but I kept watching out the window. When we finally landed at our house, he said softly, It will all be OK, kiddo. She'll be fine. And you know, it was good to cry sometimes. To be sad. In the rear-view mirror, I caught his eyes, swollen and glassy, and I knew that he wanted me to bawl, he longed for me to cry and cry and cry. But I wouldn't grant him that. I unbuckled my belt and rushed to my room. And once there, I dropped to the floor and begged whoever was in charge that in the morning I would no longer have a mother. I didn't want her to die, rather I wished for her to disappear from my life, like how Santa simply vanished once the truth had leaked. When I told Terry about my mam, he said his dog got dosed with cancer and had to be put down.

We both stepped back from the bonfire in wild expectancy but after a moment, when nothing happened, I kicked Terry. You lit it wrong, I said. Terry bent down and instructed me to do the same. I still couldn't see anything and was about to kick Terry again when he pointed at a small wavy light. A peach-orange bulb flickering. Terry said we had to feed it fast, so we poured the rest of the lighter fuel directly over this light. On our hunkers, we watched the flame grow and stretch and spread like skinny, witchy fingers. We stood as smoke, thick and black, started to balloon over the field.

In our base, Terry explained to me how his dog, Sam, was seven years old when he got the cancer. He spoke to the floorboards about how much he loved that dog and I didn't say a thing, no sorrys, no nothing. I had never heard anything that resembled affection from Terry before, and I probably believed he wasn't capable of love or of even understanding the word in the way I did. He was marked and different to me, lesser. What did he know? What could a knacker know? I picked up a stick and played with it as Terry explained how his dog started puking up its food and sleeping all day and stopped wagging his tail. Sam had always wagged his tail, even when he was tired, even when he was being given out to, Sam wagged his tail. Terry looked at me and I didn't meet his eye as I passed the stick from one hand to the other. Terry said he went to the vet despite his father telling him what was going to happen. The vet's room was cold, and they lay Sam flat on a steel table. Here, Terry quietened for a moment, his breathing heavier. I didn't stir. I didn't say, It's alright, Terry. I chewed the inside of my mouth. There was no difference between his story and mine, but I wanted nothing more than to hear a voice shouting my name, calling me in, calling me away. He continued, after roughly rubbing his nose, and said the last thing he remembered was Sam's tail pounding the table. Pounding the table as he walked out of the room.

My eyes itched as treacle and red scraped at the sky. We inched further back as the bonfire crackled and let out a drawly groan. The pallets had crumbled to crud. The tyres were dripping. Yellow sparks burst forth into life and jittered around us like midges. It was beyond our control, the bonfire, we both knew that, but my teeth didn't chatter, my legs didn't tense to run. I spat out the taste of burning and watched on.

I faked innocence in the weeks after her death. Waking my father at night so he'd stand guard for ghosts as I went to the bathroom; his naked ass two crescent moons in the doorway. I asked him continuously, Where did Mam go? As if I believed she might have popped to the shops. Over dinner I'd get him to recount in detail the wonders of heaven. One evening, Mark grabbed me afterwards in the hall. His face as ugly as I ever seen it. He said to me, She's dead. Mam is dead. That was it. I jokingly asked Terry, Where's my mam? He pointed at the sky, twirling his index at some unidentified spot. He said, She is up there with Sam. In the stars or something. The idea warmed me, but I laughed at him. You need to grow up, Terry, I blurted. My mam is dead. She is rot in the ground. And then I said it again: You need to grow up, you dirty knacker. Nothing else was said after that and I eventually invented an excuse so I could escape home early. See you tomorrow, Terry said.

Our skin glowed albino pale beside the bonfire. Parts of me were already scabbing like brittle paint on wood. By now the field was scalded, the grass and bracken black. Terry coughed and gagged, his cheeks puffing with sick. I watched clots of garnet dance on his sleek forehead.

During the service I focused on the coffin. I sensed the pressing cup of my dad's palm around my shoulder and my auntie's pats on my knee and the army of outstretched hands, but I kept my gaze locked on the wooden box. And during the drinks afterwards, my brother stole me from the arcade machine to go get food. He gave me a piggyback to the chipper van, and we sang songs Mam had once sang to us. At the chipper, he asked what I wanted. I said a burger and I assumed he'd remember my loathing for onions and red sauce. But when the bun arrived jampacked with both I didn't complain. I ate and listened as Mark told stories about Mam from when I was a baby, about her taking us to see the dolphin in Kerry, about me ruining a trip to the circus over the clowns, about her dressing us up as Batman and Robin one Halloween. All fairy tales, as unreal as mine and Terry's games. Burgers finished, we balled our tinfoil into a bin and Mark told me then that I was a good lad. I thought I should say the same, but I didn't.

The bonfire began fanning out, burning the hedges and fences, sweeping hungrily into other fields. I imagined the surrounding sheep and lambs being roasted, their demented baaing, their alien eyes rolling white. Embers popped around our ears, blasting themselves into nothing. Sweat furred my back. From over my shoulder, Terry called my name. I stepped further forward, the heat hitting like a punch. Already gummy blisters were scalping the flesh on my arm, bubbling there, the colour of dribbling varnish. That close to the fire, I could glimpse sprays of rust and red and soot. I could hear only this grasshopper rattle.

Terry was at the back of the church during the funeral. He was the only one who waved. I pretended not to see him and clung to my auntie as she steered me along.

I bounced closer until the bonfire was almost touching me. And in an instant, I reached for it. Fierce pain coursed through my right arm. The heat clawing through bone, wiry nerves, and skin. I saw colours, bright, throbbing colours, and then Terry grappled himself around my stomach and suplexed us away from the fire. Atop me, Terry screamed my name, sweat sliding down his horrified face. My arm was like an object beside me. It seemed bound in clingfilm and already yellowed hoops of it were peeling – the flesh stripping to a savage, wet pink that was sticky as flypaper. I smelled grilled meat. My breath roared. Terry cried my name again and shambled onto his feet. He ran and I followed.

We decided to light the bonfire on the last night of our holidays. We spent the day before checking over our supplies. Inspecting everything while clogging our noses against the musky decay. It was a cloudless afternoon and I was shivering by the time we were done. When we stood with our bikes at the galvanised gate – where I'd blow left and him right – I thought I should say something. Thank him. Tell Terry I owed him one, though I didn't know what exactly I owed. Tell him he was my best friend. But every time I tried to gather those words and arrange them into order, they wouldn't float out correctly from my mouth and so I was left to just look at him, not smiling, not doing anything. Terry moved his hands from his pockets to behind his back, his body slightly swaying. Without a word, he then jumped onto his bike and began pedalling. I don't recall how long I stood there, alone amongst the silhouettes of our world, listening to the near-silent swish of his wheels as they tore through darkness.

We sprinted. Barely touching damp grass and reed as we hopped a drainway and then leaped ourselves over a fence. The bonfire a giant behind us. Our feet burned cool against the concrete as we came onto the Sound Road. I could taste the air again, zesty and fresh. From somewhere, a siren blared. We flew on towards my door.

The night of the funeral, I walked in on my father crying on the toilet. He was in his white shirt but wore no pants, only underwear. His bare legs were pudgy with matted black hair like Velcro. I didn't speak and I didn't turn around, and, finally, he got up and washed his hands. While drying them on a towel, he said, The show must go on, kiddo.

My brother was in the porch, a phone against his ear. My father beside him, shouting, Did you see the fire? We hurtled past them to my bedroom. I unlatched my window, pushing it open, and shimmed up to the windowsill. Terry yelled, Hurry on, as he struggled after me. On my tippy-toes, I grabbed hold of the gutter and Terry boosted me onto the roof. He then pulled himself up.

I felt like we could see everything from up there, the Sputnik television aerials, the hills, the disordered houses, the bogs, all flattened out in front of us. The bloated stink of smoke had wafted down from the fire, along with ginger petal-shavings which drifted lazily in the air, and in the distance, we saw the blue glare of Garda cars. Terry clutched my good hand and we sat there all night, sobbing out sweat, our bodies thawing the frosted slates. We watched jets of water tear into the flames, watched stooped figures shovel dirt onto steaming ditches, watched the tip of our bonfire reach out one last time for the stars, before failing and falling in on its own shadow. By then the blush of dawn was spreading far across the horizon and sunlight was breaking against the burnt out field. The last sparks of our bonfire fading alongside the night. Terry's hand shook in mine. A great spasm of pain flared in my dead arm. Together, we watched the bonfire perish into black.

# Pure Gold

I was glue-lipped, dangling on the border between the horrors and the thirst. We were out in Ziggy's yard, huddled on the lichen-knackered backstep as the sun bate down. The air was close and muggy, like someone else's breath. Beside me Ziggy moaned, his head in bowed arms, the grease on his mop of hair blinding. The early giddiness we shared had dried and now an ashy staleness flowered. We grunted, we mourned. Pressed against my front teeth – furry in their unbrushed state – I felt the lunar, sour bumps of my tongue, still tasted the sick-spittle which had caked the hinges of my lips, still reeled from the fear of last night. I was seventeen, the Leaving a swelling shadow behind me.

I pounded the cooked patio with my feet. Felt my cheek, grooved like a peach from the shabby floorboards where I had scooped out a couple of hours. Above was streaked blue, so divinely blue you'd believe in angels, so bright you couldn't glance at it and not shudder. The hedges and the browning grass purred under the heat. The windows and the fidgety insects shimmered. And amongst this hazy backdrop, I could hear the distant shearing of every make of lawn on the Island: the thistle fields, the reed-swamps, the block front gardens. 'Fuck this,' I said. 'Fuck this completely.'

'Proper cuntish weather,' Ziggy said, flapping a hand at his neck. His plaid shirt was turbaned over his head. He lifted himself up a little before crumbling again. The sun hadn't tanned him as much as scabbed his skin, crisped it the colour of fried bacon. 'It's not natural. I'm telling you, we aren't made for it,' Ziggy said. 'This heat.'

I mumbled, continued tracing with my limp finger the grikes between each slab in the patio. In sections, dog-tongued dock leaves had forced their roots through cement. Growing like pubes between the flagstone. I admired their perseverance. I coughed, spat a small sack of sick. The fry had done no good.

'It's not right,' Ziggy said. 'Not natural. If we kept this weather half the year, the country'd be goosed.' He raised a coaxing brow at me. 'Wouldn't it?'

'Jesus, I'm dying,' Ziggy said. He swung wide his knees and then pushed himself to his feet. 'Really dying.'

He bullfooted a nearby football. I watched as it rolled, rolled, rolled into a bush. He moved towards the open French doors, where just inside we had stacked our plates. Three or four horseflies suckled on the smeared remains and it smelled something rotten. From near the plates, Ziggy reached for a lip-smudged glass. I watched him closely. I always hated how he drank, the sickly glug and gargle of it. The bob of his Adam's apple like some fat arse slumping down the mattress of the bunk bed above you. Ziggy was bok-eyed – the nickname self-proclaimed in first year before others got creative – and all paste and bones. In comparison to his elastic limbs, even my body seemed heroic. Worst of all though was Ziggy's hole. Due to misshapen ribs and a bollixed sternum – he wasn't sure of the actual cause himself – there was a pothole indentation bang in the middle of Ziggy's chest. A crater that was wider than my fist. It was like the gaping impact of a punch, like his body had caved in. He said I was the only one he had ever shown it to. Trusted enough. In May, when he first told me about Marian – about them – I had whispered, straight off, about his hollow. I scrunched my toes and enquired how did he hide it from her? Sternly he explained how he kept a hand tucked under the front of his T-shirt. His arm went numb from keeping the T-shirt tugged down. I said she must have noticed. She must have felt the void on his chest like when you miscount the steps on a darkened stairway. She must have been freaked by it. From the slit of his mouth, Ziggy asked, 'When you going to get it done?'

I cut apart a dock leaf with my thumbnail. Once more, I saw her leading me to the fire escape. My hand in hers. I saw her sit on the third chrome step, one heel planted on the first. Her skirt hacked above the knee so that I could make out tiny pinkish bumps along her thigh. I winced, turning colours again.

'What you reckon?' I said abruptly.

Ziggy widened his eyes and then collapsed once more onto the step, his head falling between his knees.

'Ziggy.'

He crooked an elbow over his eyes. Shrugged his shoulders towards the sun. Murmured, 'Fucked if I know, Dicey.'

We were in the midst of our summer. When for two weeks the place was scorched. Roads were full of oily mirages. Keel prom was slapped with sandaled-feet and the hopscotch dribbles of ice cream cones. Casey's Well in Dooega had dried to plain earth. Yachts puzzled our waters. The Island twitched and throbbed with heat and we had to endure.

'Cans?' I said. 'Rollover?' I wanted to write off last night.

'Yeah?' Ziggy said with a hitch in his voice.

'Nothing better to do.'

'Right,' Ziggy said. 'Right, you see, I'm tight on money is the only thing.'

I stuck my hand into my pocket, fished out my wallet. A hand-me-down from the brother, Barzo. I teased through it – a wishful condom, a business card from a club I hadn't gone to in Castlebar – and scraped out a ratty twenty. Ziggy's jaw sagged to one side. I needed him and his date of birth.

'Come on, you poof,' I said.

He threw back his head. Seemed to be considering the inner workings of the world, the billions of stars in the sky, the waste and bone and treasure buried below us, before he sighed, 'Fuck it so.'

Ziggy stumbled upstairs to change and I wandered to the front of the house. Taking in mouthfuls of air. A cat hid under the exhaust end of a car, a fat tabby. I spooked it with a stomp. Grass blew white in the sun and, crouched against the wall, I scanned through my messages. The skin around my thumb beginning to bleed as I scrolled down. Four texts from Tracy, messy with question marks. She went to school in Westport: reddish blonde hair, braces with these gold elastic bands. I bent for a rock and flung it into a thorn bush across the way. Dust rose, floury as a baker's clapped hands. Then I heard Ziggy's footfalls and I quickly learned each text off by heart and deleted them one by one. I stood. Ziggy had thrown on a hoodie, despite the heat.

'Story,' he said. There was a sheen to his face, I guessed he had ran it under the tap.

We glided down to Sweeney's. Our post-mortem of last night interrupted only by fits of shirking laughter. The rattled pain forgotten as we bit into the raw shape of the day. In the dusty fields you could hear the cattle, their club hoofs crushing the reedy grass. I told Ziggy about a heifer who had collapsed and died out near Keem Lake. Its owner, out on the piss since the sun exposed itself, hadn't filled the trough in a week. I told him how a pack of stray dogs had savaged the cow's body and when a neighbour finally went to clear the carcass, she found the other cows nosing and tonguing up the heifer's dark blood.

'Why'd you bother telling me that?' Ziggy asked.

Before the main road, when the briars stopped strangling the path, he mentioned Tracy. Casually, tactically. He knew I'd been after her, I had informed him that some mutually beneficial deal had been arranged. He said he saw me go off with her last night. Did I finally?

'Yeah,' I lied. Ziggy glanced at me then fixed his stare onto the road. 'I went off with her. Out the back of the club. You know the spot there?'

'Fair play,' he said. 'That's the first time done so.'

Cutting him off, I asked about Marian.

'What about her?' His forehead crinkled.

'Just I caught her last night with Jamesy. You know, the tall lad from near Mulranny?' I didn't speak for a moment. 'Did you see that, too?'

He nodded. Spat and called her something.

We followed along the bank of the main road towards the Sound, cool in the shade of high shrubs. The church bell bonged and I told Ziggy you could nearly hear the shutters of the offie being rolled open for us. 'It's like our love song,' I joked.

Ziggy smirked with a loud tssk, but didn't face me.

By Brett's shop, the scaffolding still framed around the crumpled chimney, we passed Martin Cooney and his father. Mr Cooney had a hand cradled under Martin's elbow, a paper stuffed under the other. Martin turned away from us. It was known that Martin was home and unmasked but this was our first glimpse. To us now he was only the half-moon piece fashioned by that wicked slash of glass. The bridge of his nose, right eye socket and cheek were divided into three distinct Africa-shaped sections. Stitches ran between his nose – inflamed like a Mr. Potato Head piece – and his lips, and the skin around these cuts was dabbed a sponge-cake yellow. Most shocking to me though was the shakiness in Martin's eyes, as if these globes belonged not to a fancy college boy but to an eighty-something-year-old, lost and afraid.

'Boys,' Mr Cooney said. We nodded, keeping our heads low, but glared back once we crossed to the church side of the road. Standing under a roof of fuchsia, we watched as Mr Cooney almost folded Martin into the backseat of their car.

'He got a bad going over,' I said. 'From the McNultys.' The perfume of incense wafted by.

'Yeah,' Ziggy paused. 'Pricks.'

Outside the wrinkled church gate, a crew of bundled-up sleeves had assembled. Smoking and chatting. They must have slipped out after Communion.

'That's what you should have done last night,' I said.

'What you mean?'

'To James. When you seen him groping Marian.' A sly, ugly grin spread across my face. 'That's what you should have done to him.'

'Would you leave it?'

I clipped his heel and sped to match his pace. 'I'm only messing, Ziggy. Relax.'

'Piss off,' he said quietly.

We powered on and crossed over to Sweeney's. By a chain of trolleys, I handed him my twenty. 'Get two eight packs, yeah?' I ordered. 'That should do us plenty.'

'Sound.' Ziggy brushed a hand through his hair, pocketed the money with a clenched fist. He then double tapped his arse-pocket.

'Go on so,' I slouched onto the kerb. 'You don't need me to hold your hand.'

Left alone, I huffed and placed my phone flat between my feet. The scene around me was noise. Radios and blaring tunes and fisted honks – the towners not wide to the ingenious notion of letting your car run as you nipped into the shop. There was the moil of the ice cream machine and the shouts of kids in unseen gardens. The front windows of the square terraced houses were wide open, releasing the crackle of the mid-afternoon Westerns, and, out the back, you could hear the winged flap of sheets, pegged neat and fatly on washing lines like flocks of neck-wrung geese. Cars licked bumpers on the road, surfboards on their roof racks – the sand from yesterday still gritty on the shark fins. A tractor spurted black smog like a trumpet.

I watched motionless, my stomach boiling once more, considering if I wanted to puke or not, until there, in the cramped backseat of a Peugeot, I spied a girl. Her lips puckered. Her wispy hair so white it looked like it'd sting to touch. Her driver beeped. His flexed arm, carpeted with black hairs, rested on the open window. He wore sunglasses without shame. He gestured something to the girl, who, grinning, leaned forward and kissed his chin and its dirty stubble. I could almost taste their smell. She linked her arms around his neck and let her fingers stroke his chest. Then her hand dropped further and I imagined where it went. I turned to my phone and looked up again only to give his licence plate the finger and watch as his car, and the hundreds of other cars, rolled on towards a beach that I'd never see in the same way they did. That icy fear of the morning-after slithered back: Why does summer always feel like it belongs to someone else?

I thought about Tracy. With a shudder I replayed us scudding through the fire exit. Her heels – red velvet with peeping-Tom toes – barking against the gravel as we moved. Her ringlets had frizzed from the heat of the club, and she brushed one slowly, ever so slowly, behind her shoulder. I heard the tap-tap-tapping of her heel on the metal step. I saw her smile, those small cubic fangs, like baby's teeth. I groped my cock, soft and hopeless, and watched her face change to a frown and then mortified confusion. Her voice calling after me, the confident twang abandoned, 'What's wrong with you? Mark. Come back. Mark, don't leave me here. Please!'

The shakes had returned, my leg vibrating against the curb. I hawked out a toffee-ball of mucus. I wanted to tell her how I felt, blame nerves or whatever, and then beg her to keep it fastened between us. I wanted to rush back, tell her why. I picked up my phone then dropped it down again. But I also saw how nakedly I only wanted to hide it, say she ran off on me. Say she was the one who fled in gop-mouthed panic. It was her fault. I bent forward and tried to make out the Peugeot, but it was long gone, swallowed by the blur. Who would ever know? An ant wandered over my phone's screen. I watched its struggle, each leg moving like it was cranked forward. Then with the coarse side of my thumb, I smeared it into nothing. I cleaned the thumb on the hot concrete as a shout came from behind.

Ziggy held two golden packs like firewood. Eight cans in each. I took one and inspected it. 'You didn't fuck up anyway,' I said.

'Where we head?' Ziggy ignored me and slipped down between the metal bars. 'Maybe under the bridge?'

I eyed the sun. 'Be lit down there.' Heavenly, the cold beers dampened the underside of my shirt. 'We wouldn't be able to cope.'

'Where so?'

We started walking back the way we came. Weighing spots – strengths and weaknesses and if others might have already got there. By now the church had cleared out but the smell of candles lingered. I suggested the ball alley near Lavelle's. Ziggy reminded me of the walk and the ordeal of hitching. 'Not worth it,' he said.

'The Swamp,' Ziggy said and stopped. I kept going. 'Dicey. What about the Swamp?'

I leant my head from side to side. It was a good suggestion and this annoyed me.

'Where else is there? I'm not walking in this,' Ziggy said. He knew he had the upper hand. 'Besides, it's only over the road.'

We doubled back and diverted, via the beer garden of The Clinic, to the lane that bent along the library. The sun was now in front of us, a flipped copper penny. The tarmac sizzled and the far end of the road was brushed utterly blank in this heavy light.

'This heat.' Ziggy stuck out his tongue.

The ache was gnawing again in the corners of my head. I was parched and the cans were now a burden rather than a gift. I lifted high my pack and said in a mock biblical gasp, 'My cross to carry.' Ziggy laughed and I added with a bump of his shoulder, 'Seriously, we need to tuck into these boys soon.'

Ziggy agreed and half-started a sentence but drew it back. He then said, 'Look, what happened with Tracy?'

'What happened with *Tracy*?' I mimicked.

'Don't get like that. I just heard something. I heard from—'

'I told you what happened.' He was trying to wound and I stared blindly ahead. 'I told you, didn't I?'

'Dicey, come on,' he said. 'You can tell me.'

Then, when we were halfway down the road, Ziggy muttered, 'Watch.'

I squinted, my cheeks burning, and recognised the unmistakable headstone frame of Declan Coyle. He was sat on a wall, a good throw from us. A phone blasting choppy rap music beside him. He was in American blue jeans and a wife-beater, mesh-like in the sun. Beside Declan, pressed against the wall, was his cousin Con McSweeney from Castlebar.

'We head back?' I noticed the quiver in Ziggy's voice. He had always been the easy prey. With his hair, his needle legs, his smarts in the classroom.

'No.' I looked more closely. They hadn't seen us yet. Four years older, they knew power, held no fear of what we did. I gave a smack of my lips. 'No, fuck that,' I said. Ziggy frowned, pleaded again, but I strode on. I faked a swagger in my steps, wanting to show Ziggy. Con whistled and Declan swung his loaf-of-bread neck our way. Against Ziggy's unease, I was sure-footed.

'The two faggits,' Declan shouted. He hopped from the wall, his features glowing. On Declan's thick upper arm was a tattoo of a Celtic cross. Black ink with green highlights. He got the tattoo done while still in school and the next day, before the morning bell, he summoned everyone, even us juniors, to the basketball court, where he unbuttoned his sleeve and tensed his bicep. I remember I felt like applauding, I remember being jealous of everything he had.

I slowed to a stop.

'What ye up to?' Declan sneered. In the right corner of his lips was a cold sore, crusted over like a dunghill. In his hand, a plastic goon in which there were only a few rusted squirts left. He whisked the neck of the bottle, his face gurning, and drained the last drips of cider. 'Well?' He threw the goon into the thickets.

'The boys have drink, Dec.' Con winked at me and my stomach turned. There was a dash of toilet-cleaner blonde in Con's fringe, and when he dragged a hand across his mouth I saw a ring on his middle finger. A brass one, like a bottle cap.

'I seen that, alright.' Declan palmed Ziggy on the shoulder, rocking him backward. 'How you gettin on, Hare? Good? Yeah? Haven't see you in awhile.'

Ziggy didn't answer, pivoted on one foot.

'Where you going with the booze?' Con faced me.

I blinked into the glare. 'Say we'll head to the Swamp.'

Con nodded. His eyes shifted and mine followed them weakly. I wondered if he was out last night. What damage he had done. He hmm-ed, mockingly considering what I said. 'The Swamp, eh. What you reckon, Dec? You in the mood for a few in the Swamp?'

'Do the lads want our company?' Declan asked. With his thumb, he frayed open the blue-and-gold wrapper of Ziggy's cans. He gripped one free and cracked it, guzzling up the foam. Con whooped. Declan dropped the ripped shreds of the wrapper and tossed another can to his cousin. 'I know Hare here wouldn't mind sharing a few cans, anyway.' Declan shrugged a rough arm around Ziggy's neck. 'Great old buddies, me and Hare.'

'But what about this other fella?' Con caught my eye and I buckled again.

'It's sound,' I strained. 'You can come with us. Yeah.'

'Good man,' Declan pushed Ziggy forward, 'Hare will lead the way.' Declan flung a can back at me. More golden scraps of the wrapper fell. Con crashed his can against mine, instructed me to drink up.

At the end of the road we jumped a gate and hiked through a field – its hay brittle like chin hair. Only the cousins talked – their tongues raking through each word. I could tell they were already long on it. After climbing another gate, we came to the slant of rock and gorse which led down to the Swamp.

In this heat, the Swamp was baked solid and hard underfoot. The grass singed my fingers, a ready spark. A pit was dug out in the centre, filled with charred wood and the tinfoil containers of DIY barbeque sets. On the opposite side was an overarching expanse of thick bog dune. Violently purple heather furred over the ridge of the dune, a sort of canopy, leaving a shadow on the brown water; the wiry bone-roots of a nearby apple tree, wind-kicked as an old hag, crawled in and out of the dune's crust like barky stalagmites. I had the sudden sensation of being watched, judged, and I quickly finished my can. I flaked my empty at the dune and clumps of grey earth dropped free, smashing into the water.

Declan took the eight-pack from Ziggy. 'You're good for something anyway, Hare.' Declan dropped the pack by the pit, snatched one out and then, after jerking his arm back twice, passed Ziggy a can. 'You wormy little shit.'

Con stood beside me, peering into the stream. He spat out a drooping yo-yo of saliva. 'Not a bad spot.' He pretended to punch me, before laughing. 'Throw us another there, Dec.'

Declan slumbered into the shade and we sat more or less in a line next to him. By now our cans were heated, the freezer cold sweated from them. The beer tasted bitter and metallic and cheap but I sucked it back. Con asked who was the brains that thought of this place? Declan pushed down Ziggy's head, said it wasn't Hare anyway. Ziggy hadn't spoken more than a sentence since they found us and I knew I had stung him. Con kicked me.

'Must be Einstein here, so.' I smirked but didn't reply.
'Some man,' Con said.

We drank steadily from then. The sun battering our
exposed shins. The stream whistling by. Con and Declan
talked, seemingly forgetting about us until Declan
requested a fresh can and either myself or Ziggy would get
up and hand it to him. I concentrated on getting drunk,
rapidly dismissing everything but the can snug between
my legs, the measured sips and the tales being smacked
about. Declan boasted about scabbing a tidy lump from
the off-hours offie in The Island Head. 'Made a clean
grand last month. Cash.' While Con recounted – without
looking at any of us – how he took a bird last night. The
details eerie, making me hold my breath. 'She was wet as
a rag.' He repeated this again, his hushed voice scrawling
like a razor blade against chalkboard. He told us where it
had happened and how he came after his final drawn-out
pump, his hand thumping the beat into the ground.

When Ziggy's pack was empty, the gold wrapper was
lobbed into the stream. We tore open mine and drank on
and on and on.

Overhead, a white line ripped through the blue seams
of the sky. I slurped my can, blowing a hair of grass from
the lid, and watched it. I wagered saying something,
pointing out the plane – was it even a plane? 'Hare, my ol'
buddy?' Declan said, loudly, and adjusted his body so he
faced Ziggy. His tattoo and bicep tensed, 'I meant to ask,
you still a virgin?'

Con clapped hand against thigh.

I took a drink, forgot about the plane. Ziggy vaguely responded.

Declan cupped his ear, bent closer to Ziggy. 'What was that? Speak up, Hare. I can't hear ya.'

'I'm not,' he said.

'Are you sure?' Declan said.

'He doesn't sound sure,' Con said.

'Are you a virgin, Hare?' Declan asked again. I grinned when Declan eyed me. 'Come on. We're all pals here.'

'I'm not,' Ziggy shouted.

'Oh. Go easy, Hare,' Declan howled. 'I believe you, I believe you.' Ziggy shot a look at me. I realised he still hadn't finished his first can.

'What about his buddy, Dec,' Con yelled. A whiff of a breeze crossed. Enough to ward off midges. 'Is he a virgin and all, do you think? Is there a pair of them in it?'

'I'm not.' I took a long sip and held in my gut, tried to sound confident. 'I'm really not.'

'A right slayer, I bet,' Con said.

'Who'd you pipe?' Declan asked me. 'Remember now, the right hand is no good, Dicey.'

I scoffed a laugh and messed again with my shirt. The stream glistened pure gold. 'I was with Tracy Keating. I was with her.'

'Ivan Keating's youngest one?' Declan said. 'With the braces?'

'Where you take her?' Con snapped.

'Yeah. Her.' My throat felt clogged. I shook my can.

'Ziggy's gaff. He had a free one, so took her back. Did it in Ziggy's house then.'

'Man, Dicey,' Declan's voice trailed off. He flung a can into the stream, shattering it. A dragonfly danced by, its wings rainbows in the light, and for a moment, I concentrated on that, the beautiful colours. Until, as an afterthought, Declan added, 'You got more action in that house than my man Hare, anyway.'

Ziggy shifted beside me but didn't speak. We caught eyes and he looked away. I shook my can a little harder, brought it to my lips. I knew if the places were changed, if he was the one telling tales, I'd rat him out. As fast as anything. I'd rat him out. I'd make him the joke. I'd make him suffer. Now, I prayed he wouldn't do the same. I prayed that he would be better than me.

'Two slayers on our hands, Dec. We could learn a thing or two from them.' Con smiled. One of his front teeth was uneven. Bent, as if you could just twig it out. 'I'd say they give the women a good seeing to. Leave them feeling wake.'

'Tell us how you do it, lads,' Con continued. 'Tell us what you do to them.'

Declan laughed.

'Go on, show us your moves, lads,' Con shouted. 'Stand up and show us how you do it.'

The shadow from the heather behind had crept further along our thighs. The sun wheeling backwards. I was being strung up again. 'I always wondered how Hare managed to do it,' I said. 'With the hole in his chest.'

'What's this about? What hole?' Declan's ears perked. 'What's wrong with your chest, Hare?'

'Show them, Ziggy.' I saw what I was unravelling but I couldn't stop. I didn't want to stop. I feared more what they could reveal. Ziggy mouthed my name. I knew what I was doing. 'Go on, show them,' I said.

'Hare,' Declan lugged himself up. 'Are you keeping secrets from me. I thought we were friends?' Declan went for Ziggy's top. 'There's no secrets between friends, Hare.' Ziggy kicked at Declan's grasp and struggled to his feet. 'Fuck away from me,' Ziggy screamed. Declan tried to choke him into a headlock but again Ziggy managed to scramble free, his legs doing ninety, but then Con rushed in, tackling Ziggy to the ground. The rustle of grass, a punch was thrown. Together, the cousins wrenched off the hoodie, revealing the soft skin which the sun hadn't itched, revealing that smooth, hairless hemisphere. They howled and I howled with them. Ziggy tried to stagger away but tripped over the pit, falling in arse-first, his hands locked together hoping to hide his chest. Con burst into Muttley-hysterics. I passed Ziggy's hoodie to Declan, who threw it into the ash of the pit.

'Fuckin cunts,' Ziggy stumbled up. His voice wobbled. I looked at the stream. 'Fuck you cunts.' He ran.

We toasted to Ziggy's chest. Con and Declan shouted new insults and names for Ziggy's hole. I kept quiet, smiled, nodded when it was expected, and shied away from the glimpse of who I was. The laughter carried us for a while.

'Last orders,' Con shouted in the manner of an English landlord. 'Just the three cans left.'

'That's all?' Declan pounded his fist into his palm. 'We need more drink,' he said, challenging us. Declan hooked his can at the stream. 'Need to start some proper drinking.'

'Hear, hear,' Con said.

I gave a drowsy cheer – a belch stuck forever in my throat.

Rapidly plans were pieced together. Declan named women, sent a flurry of texts and then couldn't sit still. Con mentioned pubs, potential lock-ins. I thought of crawling home when Declan turned to me, 'Dicey. You're in for the long haul, right?' I nodded, a little drum roll in my chest. 'Good, you'll lend us a few bob then. I'll source the drink.' He took my last tenner and counted what change I had – lifting each coin to the sun.

'Get a move on so, Dec?' Con began rolling a joint. 'I'll stall here with this bruiser.'

'Right. Sound.' Declan glanced at me before hurrying off.

Con lit the joint. I nursed my can, holding it to my lips without letting any of it trickle down my throat. Pretending to myself there was a reason we weren't talking. The battered tree moved a little in the late afternoon wind, and beneath it, apples lay like hardened nuts, rank and spoiled. His voice came to my ears as a scratch. 'Tell us the truth, you've never been with a woman, have you?'

'What?' I said. My voice pitched. 'Didn't I tell you about Tracy?'

He sucked the joint. Exhaled a spiral spell of smoke. 'You told us that alright, but.' There was a glint in his eye. 'But I could smell the horseshit.'

I sifted grass with my fingers.

He laughed – not with venom, that lone 'Ha' – but with some tone of understanding. He leaned back, his right elbow propping him. 'No shame in it.' The stream ran all the way down from Slievemore, tracked through briar bushes, through this field, and onward still to the sea. 'They are tricky, the women.'

At the bottom of the stream I spotted the royal blue of our discarded cans. Near it, one of the gold wrappers was caught in a leafless briar. I stared at this and asked when he had first done it.

I heard him smile. The sap breaking as his lips opened. 'Lost mine when I was fourteen,' he said. 'To a neighbour from up the road. This ol' one. She asked me one morning, when I was going to the shops for my mother, would I call over?' He clicked his fingers. 'Just like that.'

'Good?' I asked. A question unsure if it was even a question.

He said nothing. Then after a while, 'Yeah. She knew the ropes alright.'

I didn't dare look at him. My eyes focused instead on the sheath of plastic. I tugged at myself. The sun spiked right through it.

'I've done it with others as well,' he said. 'Different folks,' he paused. 'You'd like to try it someday, ah?'

'Yeah.'

He laughed to himself, rose. He stamped on his joint – its smell oozed – and struggled over a bush. I listened to him piss. The stiff hiss of it as it hit the hay stalks. The passing of gas and his chuckle after.

Con stepped out. 'What are you smiling at?' He swiped grass from his boots. His shirt was off and he had left his fly and belt undone. There was a dark stretch of hair diving from his bellybutton to the band of his boxers. I watched him groom himself, hearing the jangle of his bracelet. The tinker gold of it. 'Some heat,' he said.

My hand tore at the grass and I felt muck under my nails. 'We could swim.'

'A doggie-paddle, is it?' He laughed but then stopped. 'Could be nice, all right. What you think? Could be nice.'

I didn't reply. But carefully nodded. I heard his body – the old man crack of his bended leg – as he pushed further down his jeans. He let out a grunt as he pulled a sock off. Through the distant fir trees the wind blew as if gossiping. I fingered the laces of my shoe. Felt the dampness under my arm.

'I won't tell,' he said as he passed me.

He balanced a foot on a large mossy rock and then let himself fall into the stream. His boxers baggy and tartan. He had moles on his back, connecting dots. Wires of hair grazed on the cove of his neck. I unsnapped my belt. Lashed it out from the jean buckle. I laid my shirt neatly on the spread-legged jeans. Straightened my back.

The stream was about seven-foot wide and bracing cold, though the day was too hot for it to really freeze us. My feet rested on slime and stone. I rubbed my hand along my arms, where the line of sun-rash and freckles met, and cupped some water onto my shoulders and the unbroken chest that had saved me. 'It's nice,' I ventured.

In the deepest area, the water came just above my hip. We ducked ourselves in, let the liquid peel over our shoulders. Hunched in the brown water, Con's body took on a different shape. It was oily and runny. I thought I could scrub it away.

'Some heat,' Con said, and he slapped a skim of water at me. I smiled, not able to laugh. My teeth chattering. I looked again at the gold wrapper, caught in the briars a little ways past us. I bounded towards it. My hands raised and poised to pare it free.

'What're you doing,' Con called. 'Where you think you're off to?' He splashed close to me and snagged my hand. Cuffed it as if we were playing a game. The ripples of his movement broke against my own like the last spin of a record.

'It's nice, the water,' he said. 'You need it on a day like today. Don't you need it?'

'Yes,' I whispered.

A trickle of sweat escaped from my temple and pricked my eyelid. I felt him behind. His pelvis pressing against my back. He didn't bother turning me. I watched the water, noticing how it was fleshed in its movements, noticing our reflection, and I let my hand dash this away just as his thumb flicked at my underwear. I felt winded as the stream broke against me, against us, as my blood strengthened. He groaned, 'Easy.' I shut my eyes to the sun, but its rays were still visible. These shiny green discs. My breath circled above while his heaved against my sleek neck. I sniffed the air like a dog. I trembled and then I didn't.

I opened my eyes, suspended and drifting atop the stream, my own milky self. 'There you are.' He bit the lobe of my ear. 'There you are.'

His arms wrapped around my stomach and guided me until we were again in the middle of the stream. 'Now,' he said. I fought for a moment but he held his forearm against my lower back. I bridged my arms in front of me and the water came to my elbows. I heard the sound of spit. I gritted my teeth and saw myself as if from afar. I felt the pleasure as if from afar. Then I heard a voice. Declan's. Raring towards us. I thought I heard the echoes of others too. Con thrusted forward and I swung an elbow, hard. Connected first with his stomach and, spinning, his dodgy front tooth. It cut into the skin between my knuckles.

My underwear was sodden and I pulled them back up. Con looked at me, his gaze hurt and glassy from the drink. His boxers were like a fetter around one leg. Blood came from his mouth. 'What's wrong?' he said. 'What's wrong?'

I stomped on his stomach. 'Get away.'

Declan ran into view. He had a dripping plastic bag roped around his wrist. 'What's going on?' I could barely make out his face against the sun.

'He tried to fuck me,' I screamed, spit spraying from my mouth. 'He tried to get me to wank him off. And he tried to fuck me.' I scampered towards the ledge. Con struggled up, purple blood now gushing from his nostril. I grabbed a rock and feinted to clock him with it. He fell again.

Declan studied me and then his cousin. He shushed us and let down the bag, already tattered. On my own beating chest, I felt the hard and brutal light of the day. With a pointed finger, Declan spoke to the fallen boy, 'What did I tell you?' He bent for a rock and we both stepped forward.

# Hoarfrost

They had veered from the tarmacked run of the Glon – where she had asked him twice to slow, to keep an eye out for the left turn – and now faced west onto a slap of backroad. Annette Cafferky straightened in the front seat and squinted ahead. Beyond the glare of the headlights, there was only the polished blackness of November, broken here and there by the light of a square window, of the odd, distant car. She was nearly positive this was the road. The car chugged stubbornly along, its tyres cracking and popping against the clay. It was a biting Friday night; the air weighty. On the bushes and thorns, hoarfrost sparkled in the headlights like pluckable diamonds, and above, the night sky seemed taut, firm. 'I'm sure this is it,' Annette said, more to herself than her husband. About halfway down they came to a signpost: a network of wooden arrows and warnings for concealed entrances. Squirming a little farther forward, Annette searched and found the name of the B&B from Polly's directions. She mouthed it – Aisleim Lodge – and then said for Frank to drive on. She settled back again, content now. They were heading the right way. From here, she remembered, could practically recite, it was a straight five-mile drive to the house. 'It's only over the road,' she told him.

Tonight, Annette was going to fuck another man, and Frank was going to fuck another woman. That was what was going to happen. And she was excited, she had reminded herself of this fact throughout the afternoon, the weeks. It was a newly acquired habit of hers: the constant need to remind herself how she should feel. But she was excited for tonight. She was. She crossed her arms and then, feeling rigid, overly formal, snugged her hands between her thighs, laughed to herself. Annette was thin, a thinness hard-earned from dawn sprints, furry healthshakes, lucuma powder, a thinness which she didn't fully believe she owned. Moles peppered her arms – where the skin was papery, prone to rashes – and her hair was black, curly, and tossed now over one shoulder. She asked Frank to turn up the heat and he yanked the knob on the vent. Drips of sticky air like a cough from the rear of a hall. She didn't thank him. A cashmere scarf was spooled around her neck and she widened it and then grazed her hand along the length of her dress. She was worried it was too short. But really, what was considered too short for such an occasion? Between her knees rolled two bottles of lime-white wine. The gold cap of one unsealed, its label peeling at the corner.

The car stalled suddenly before a crossroad spangled and punched with ice.

Frank's finger kept time against the wheel and she said, faintly, 'It's straight on.' His face stirred with recognition, but he didn't acknowledge her. The car lurched forward. As the headlights washed over the ice it was for a moment dazzling, brilliantly colourful, then more like a shard of sunlight against dusty mirror. She noticed that.

Frank had barely spoken two full lines since he had learned about tonight. Throughout the week he had kept things uncomfortably civil, acting jovial rather than stinging her with deliberate silence. To the boys, he had referred to Friday as 'Mammy's party'. As if they were all in on the joke. Frank was a big man and like most big men was quick to sulk. The car passed a farmhouse, on her left, its porch light shooting orange shafts across the rutted land. A dog barked. She toyed with the idea of repeating his promise, needling him with the why, with his prominent role in it all. She understood his pride as a softening piece of fruit. She touched his thigh, held it, and tentatively inspected him; the raked nick along his jawline, the piney aftershave, and she looked then at his sleeves, folded as they were above his elbow, exposing woolly forearms. A trait she could never amend, adjust. In the mornings, the taste of sleep vile in her mouth, she would find one of those arms slung over her, groping for a boob or limp and dead. She loved the vaguely threating feel of them around her. Loved how they were awkward, as if they weren't the right fit for him. In the months she had slept alone she had found herself craving that sensation.

She swallowed her idea. There was no need to strike another nail in his wrist. He was here, that was something. Plainly.

'It will freeze tonight.'

He tilted his ear but didn't reply.

'Frank.' She stroked his upper arm, his shoulder, and casually pinched his neck. 'We'll have fun.' He gave a nod, a single nod. 'It will be fun.' She reached for her white tassel handbag – a gift from the boys and him for her birthday two years back – and opened its inner compartment.

'Why do these people have to live out in middle of fucken nowhere.' With his left hand, Frank gestured at the dashboard. His watch jangled. 'I don't understand it,' he said. 'Why not Keel? The Valley?'

She sensed his eyes pass over her but she wouldn't answer at once. She retrieved a clutch bag and put it on her lap, faking an interest in its zip before answering, coldly, 'Honestly, Frank? It's their holiday home.' She felt more annoyed than she should. 'I guess they want their privacy or something. To be near the sea, maybe. Use your imagination.' She pulled down the visor and stole a glance at him, the thick expression. She sighed. His hand was clutched around the gearstick, she patted it. His chicken-skin knuckles were swollen, bloated furrows from the years of work. He had quit school at sixteen after his father's death – struck by a car as he waddled home one night – and from then on worked hard hours. Keeping his mother afloat while building a steady name for himself as a steady man. All leading up to four years ago when he finally signed the deeds for his own garage, a little ways before Castlebar. In theory, Frank was more hands off now, letting the young bucks at it, restraining himself to the books, the orders, and the occasional major job, but most evenings he still arrived home sweated with grease, proud of his discomfort, of the ache in his lower back. 'Frank,' she said, grinning slightly, 'you've got to relax.'

'More money than brains.' His hand slipped from under hers.

She sighed again and took a lipstick from the little bag, repeating his name under her breath. Frank. Frank. Frank.

He wagged his head. 'And why do you want to clown yourself?' he said. 'You look grand as it is.'

In the small, amber-lit mirror she pressed a thumb against her cheek and frowned at the results. Then she carefully retraced her smile.

She tried to ignore him, she should ignore him.

'Just don't overdo it,' he continued. 'I'm telling you, Annette.'

The car staggered down a rocky clayway, narrower. Thick grass and dandelions, tawny in the rays of the headlights, lined the centre. 'What did you promise me?' she said. She dropped the lipstick into the bag and, craning her neck, made out a chimney. Their chimney. She wouldn't look at him.

'OK.' He shook his head. 'I know. OK. Fine.'

They were twelve years married. She used to wonder, at the beginning, if it got easier or if you stopped caring as much. She still wasn't sure what the correct answer was. 'Thank you,' she said. When they first met, below in Galway, he was as innocent. Bred on an island, he announced proudly to her, much rougher than the sticks in your neck of the world. Later, drunker, as their arms absently met, he let slip he was an innocent in every way. She told herself it was love at first touch. That she knew as soon as his brawler hands fumbled about her waist, she knew right then they were cut for each other. She would imagine Frank walking her home to the docks that first night, their fingers tangled. Not presuming he was staying over, not chancing anything, rather only making sure she got back safe and sound.

She told friends and her mother and her sister and herself this story, that he had insisted on walking her home. That it was love at first touch.

During the bad months, she had chained herself to this version of Frank, clung to it like the splintering figure at the prow of the ship. It kept her going. It stressed to her the love between them, a love which shouldn't be ripped to shreds at the first tear. A love that should be fought for, tooth and claw. She knew what the Island had to say but she didn't care. It was love at first touch.

Love.

You had to scrap for love.

The car rattled over a cattle grid. Buttery light spilled from the large front windows and blew across the newly laid grass. In this glow, the scalps of bogland that surrounded seemed even more stark. They parked behind a jeep. It had an English reg. 'Typical,' Frank said. The house was a bungalow, a box, the type littered throughout the Island. The paint on the walls was rain-beaten to a dull, fossil shade. Around the side there were two plastic chairs and an upturned table, one leg missing, and Annette thought: We own chairs like that. A twisted trunk of dark bog-wood was framed in a paved circle in the middle of the garden. 'What the fuck is that for?' Frank asked.

Annette quickly fixed again the dip of her scarf and scooped up the wine at her feet, bundling the bottles and her handbag under one arm. She decided not to take off her coat and exhaled slowly, hoping to erase any blotches on her face. She wished she had brought gum. By the front door she could already see Desmond Gallagher. She wished for something for her mouth to do. She had encountered them online, exchanging emails, meeting Polly once for coffee – where Polly reminisced over the English finding her birthname Philomena confusing – and then once more for a swiftly boozy lunch in Westport. How simple and painless it was to arrange. Surely, she thought, it shouldn't have been that easy? It was only this morning that Annette had felt this wriggling in her stomach, had the brief flash to ring and cancel. A glass of wine had helped pour away those worries. Or at least mute them. Anyway, she wanted this. She was excited.

Turning now, she caught Frank gawking at himself in the rear-view mirror. His mouth ajar, the tip of his tongue moistening his bottom lip. He didn't notice her and for a moment she watched him, saw age. In the pencil-width lines under his eyes, as if slashes from glass. In the tungsten shades which brushed through his temple. In the slight hump in his back. Yet underneath the knocks and belts of time, she could make out that first Frank too, the one she imagined begging to see her again, the one walking her home. She said his name, smiling. The warmth of the car had begun to disperse, the night's cold leaking in fast, and she believed, despite everything, that she loved this man and the two boys and the life they had securely built together. Love. It was worth keeping.

She leant over and squeezed his wrist. Frank blinked, seemed to remember who she was, what they were, and then took the keys from the ignition.

'Are we right?' he said.

'What took you so long?' Desmond called as they stepped from the car. He was a slight man with rimless glasses. His hands were half in his pockets. There was an amused simper on his face.

Frank grunted to Annette. 'Your shit directions, Dessy boy.' She hid a snigger.

Her arms already outstretched, Polly trotted from behind Desmond. She cried out their names, Annette's first and then Frank's, and kissed them both on the cheek, Frank first and then Annette, before linking her arm around Annette's. 'We've been so looking forward to this,' she said. Polly's hair was cut young – a short, claret-coloured bob – and her skin was bronzed, glittery almost. Against Polly's jeans and navy sleeveless top, Annette was conscious of her dress and heels. Then Polly said, 'Haven't we, Des? Haven't we been so looking forward to tonight?' In the distance, Annette thought she could hear the sea, this dry whoosh. Mist or smoke hung in the air like talcum powder. She felt herself shrink a little. She grinned.

In the hallway, the two men shook hands. Polly hugged Annette again and stole the wine from her. Desmond pecked a kiss and asked Annette, in mock-ceremony, 'May I relieve you of your garment, madam?' Her garment being her purple rain jacket. He had the grace of a schoolteacher, rehearsed and stiffly energetic. A man who practised a joke in his head, three or four times, before saying it aloud. For a moment, she imagined darkly his fingers dappled with chalk, but then Polly goaded Annette to do a twirl in her dress. Annette laughed a little too loudly and spun, feeling like a child. The dress hung slightly above the knee and pushed up her freckled cleavage. Polly proclaimed it gorgeous, just gorgeous, asked her where she got it – 'you must tell me' – and Desmond, hooking her jacket and scarf onto a chrome stand, whistled.

'Watch it,' Frank said and they all laughed and laughed and then Polly clapped, suggested they move towards the kitchen.

Jiggling a bottle in either hand, Desmond pretended to mishear her order of white. 'Come again?' he said, chuckling. Annette played along, forcing a giggle, until Desmond poured correctly and clinked the bottle against her glass. Desmond toasted to new friends and to a wonderful evening and they cheered. The wine tasted sour to Annette, but she gulped it back. For a while they spoke of little things – money, weather, plans for Christmas. Desmond told a selection of dirty jokes and Polly floated in and out from the stove, wearing an apron; the phrase **I *DO* More Than Just Cook** printed in bold. When Frank began his introductory lecture to Desmond about the garage, Annette allowed herself to drift and examine more closely the kitchen: how the bread was left by the toaster, the unscuffed lino floor, how the fridge held no magnets of The Simpsons or a curvy Statue of Liberty. She was trying to figure how this particular couple worked, how they functioned. She was looking at a calendar – an AIB 'Great Art' one, no biroed dates, still stuck in September, with a swab of cobwebs visible underneath it – when Desmond asked over her shoulder: Was Mrs Cafferky perhaps a Russian spy?

They had nettle soup followed by salmon drenched in leek sauce with choppings of carrot and kale. The salmon was a little burnt, gritty shavings roughening the skin, and Desmond mentioned this on three separate occasions. In the hour they ate, two bottles were polished off. At one point Desmond rose and plucked two more bottles from a railed shelf. Said, 'There's no fear of us going thirsty, folks.'

Thankfully the wine started to talk for Annette and soon Polly was swatting away her words like wasps. Annette's head lightened and she was obliged, she felt obliged, to constantly rearrange her legs – crossing and uncrossing, uncrossing and crossing. From across the table, she noticed Frank had become more animated, his language cruder. His frame sprawled in his chair as he rooted out bits of salmon in his teeth with his baby finger.

No dessert. 'We're sweet enough,' Polly shouted in from the kitchen. Annette had clapped at that.

Then Polly circled with a pot of coffee and a dish of After Eights while Desmond rasped his chair nearer to hers.

As Polly filled his cup, Frank, his hands behind his head, motioned his chin towards Annette, 'Pour herself a big one while you're at it.'

Annette waved Polly away, but Frank spoke over her, 'Don't mind my wife. She's not used to this drinking. She'll have a coffee.'

Desmond smirked.

Annette smiled at Polly and then Frank. Low orchestral music had been playing from somewhere but she couldn't hear it now. 'I'm well able to mind myself, Frank.'

'I'm just saying, love.' He met her stare, winked. He messed with the strap of his watch and said, 'I'm only looking out for you.'

Polly hoisted the pot higher, shook it, and glanced at Annette sceptically: 'Well?'

Annette lifted her cup. 'Thanks,' she heard herself say. 'Thank you.' Holding her breath, she shovelled sugar into the muddy liquid while Frank went on, 'She's not able for the wine. That's all. Not used to the big drinking.' She sank her teeth into her cheek and took a sip that burned the roof of her mouth.

Desmond spoke to her with an arm over the panel of his chair, swinging effortlessly. He had moved from the subject of rejigging electrical feeds to the arduous process of building a deck. 'The problem is getting the foundation to stick. Not to give under any great weight. You understand?' He paused, wrinkled his nose, waited for her to murmur recognition, to understand. 'The soil here is like shit, you see.' He wasn't exactly handsome, she thought. His face was lean, waxy in texture, a butty chin, and on one cheek a shrivelled pink wart. She suspected Desmond was a man who was overly diligent in bed. Who would be inquisitive after every touch, who'd say sorry throughout, treating her and every woman like they were his virgins. Not like Frank. The fang marks on her neck. The thumb-bruises trailed on her arms which she'd only discover in the shower. These acrylic purple spots. She felt a foot rub hers.

'Will we make tracks to the living room?' Desmond drank the last of his wine.

She sat on a leather couch, glass in hand, in front of the turf fire. Candles lined the mantelpiece, above which was a framed painting of a farmer and his wife praying over a desolate field – Annette recognised the painting, from a postcard or a book, but she couldn't place exactly where. There were no photographs. She could find no photographs.

Desmond asked did she want a top up. Without waiting for a reply, he filled her glass to the brim. 'Just a tipple,' he said.

'Would you leave her off,' Polly shouted, bursting into bray-laughter.

Annette sucked up the wine to stop it from spilling. She felt roasted. 'I'm no good to you passed out,' she said with a shriek and felt shy.

Polly roared laughing.

'And a drink for you, sir?' Desmond asked Frank.

Frank held out his glass. The back of his hand was a liver-spotted map. From them, Annette had always gathered the whiff of cars, or what she believed was the true scent of cars: petrol and dried motor oil and ink and cold steel. Frank supped his drink, not bothering to sit. 'There's a freeze promised tonight,' he said, and lumbered towards the curtains.

'The meteorologist.' Desmond winked at Annette.

Polly called Desmond awful.

Frank didn't acknowledge this comment. With one hand, he peeled apart the curtains and instantly, moonlight glazed his face sleet-white. There was a sheen on his lip, like he had dribbled. Annette looked again at the fire. Embarrassed by him, for him. 'Yep. It will frost bad tonight,' Frank said. 'They'd want to be out early in the morning with the salt. The council. Be treacherous otherwise.'

Polly brushed Annette's knee and slid in beside her. Beneath the coffee table, Polly straightened out her legs, tensing her long skinny legs, before folding both under her body, so that she was at a slant. Polly raised her brows and Annette smiled, pretended to yawn as she discreetly rearranged her cleavage.

'They'll need the salt anyway, that's for sure. The roads will be no good,' Frank continued. 'A real wintery night.'

'Frank, will you ever sit down,' Annette pulled a face. Why did this annoy her? What harm did it do? 'You're making us all nervous.'

'Would you give us a break,' he said under his breath.

The curtains closed.

Annette took a sip of wine, rolled her eyes and tutted as if this was a part of the act. Polly adjusted herself on the couch. Frank drained his glass and then pressed it towards Desmond.

'The meteorologist requires a refill,' Frank said.

Laughter.

They talked. Punchline monologues, gossip, interjected jokes, and a lively discussion about a murder case in the news. Long-winded, long-ago stories were then shared, with Polly explaining how she met Des. Annette barely listened, a smile frozen on her face. The television was on, though the volume was off, and her eyes lingered on the screen as Polly droned on. The evening blew into late night.

Later – an hour, two hours? – Desmond declared he was going to sneak out for a cigarette. Frisking his pockets, he asked Frank if he smoked.

'Gave them up. But.' Frank shifted in his chair and she pretended not to notice. 'But I might head out with you, anyways.' He stood, looked at no one. 'Fresh air might do us no harm.'

'Do, do.' Desmond waved the found lighter and stroked a hand along Annette's collarbone before leaving. Frank badgered out after him, tugging at his belt.

'Will they ever grow up?' Polly said as the men left, throwing her eyes to the ceiling, sniggering to herself. 'How do we do it at all?' Polly leaned forward, reached for the wine, but her grip was clumsy about the bottle's neck. Knocking it. Recoiling, Polly sniggered some more and then finally lugged the bottle upright. Wine flooded across the coffee table. Polly went again to pour; her hands stable this time. She whirled the bottle towards Annette. 'More?' she asked.

Annette nodded. Drops of the wine wept onto the cream carpet. Annette felt woozy, the wine smelt now almost antiseptic. She stifled a hot desire to down the glass. To snatch the bottle and down that too. Her fingers played with her necklace as she watched wine melt into carpet.

He was out there sparking a fag, she knew that. Another promise bent and broken. She took a drink. To give up a habit that started when he was fourteen was another way, he had told her, to prove he was willing to change. To be better. To better himself. In front of her and the boys he made a show of cutting his last pack in two. 'That's it,' he repeated. 'Last of the buggers. That's it gone now.' Yet she still tasted tobacco on his teeth; the gone-off acridness hairy to her tongue, and sniffed it hushed on his collar, and one morning, before heading for her run, she had found beaten packs stowed in the van, stashed between CD cases like a magpie's nest. She had confronted him about it and in response, he had calmly lied. The other lads smoke in work, he was only minding the packs for one of the bucks – lies that could be skinned. But Annette didn't battle back. Wouldn't. Rather she consoled herself that this was the whole truth. Love cannot be culled upon discovering the first stray threads. Love. It had to be mended and stitched. That's what she was doing; with blooded fingertips, she was stitching them together.

She pointed at the spilt wine. 'Polly, watch.'

'Oh, God,' Polly moaned.

How did Annette do it? Twelve years. She took a drink, wisely, and rubbed the rim of the glass against her cheek. It felt refreshing. She thought of Ursula Storan. Her lank red hair with lines of tin, her knifed cheeks, her body that was at least a decade older than Annette's own. She liked to picture Ursula's life. How pathetic it must be. How pointless. Liked to ask herself if Ursula had really loved Frank, if it was a compulsion, or if it was just the heat that was in it. From time to time, Annette even wondered about what would have happened if word hadn't got out – if he would have had the balls to run off with her? Would Ursula have been happy then?

Polly asked her something now. Question, statement – Annette didn't process it, only watched Polly stumble from the room. The coolness of the glass spread through Annette, and she allowed the scene to form in her mind. She had pieced it together countless times, never granting herself permission to fully crumple it. Why do we replay, restage, the very moments we wish had never occurred? It was Sunday and the house was clogged with the odour of grassy football boots. She was in the kitchen, a fried egg and toast on for Cormac, when Frank jostled through the back door. A furling lily, her favourite flower, paperclipped to his shirt pocket. Her chest sank, already bitten before the bite. He told her then. His words barely registering beyond a sound and rhythm. It was a mistake. The biggest of his life. It was only a kiss. One kiss. He was drunk. He was worried over the garage. Pressure. Money. A stupid mistake. A kiss. That woman was a stupid mistake. Annette was his everything. He promised. He loved her and the boys and their life. Together. Love. He promised. Didn't they have a good life together? He would do anything. Do anything she wanted. Please. She let the two eggs fizzle to scummy brown, listened to the spring of the toaster without stirring. Love. When Cormac had stuck his head in, asking for his brekkie, she had screamed at him to get away from her.

From others, she had heard that it had been more than a kiss. They phoned with their theatrical sympathies, their displeased tutting, before telling her it had been going on for a long while. Right under your nose the pair of them had been at it. They had been hungry for it right under your snout. Annette pulled out the cord of the phone. Took a week off work and another after that. She went to London for a bank holiday, talked to strangers and felt only sickness. Then a month later, while pushing a trolley through a noon-hectic aisle in Sweeney's, she had met her. Ursula. She wore a too-large khaki jacket, held a milk carton and she looked at Annette for a long time before walking over. Her voice snappy as a zipper as she asked how Annette was coping. Those milling around watched, a woman squeaked out a comment. Ursula shrugged the perspiring milk to her chest, and said, How are you coping, Annette? Silence and then Annette's voice croaked out that she was fine. Myself and my family are fine. Thank you very much. Glad to hear it, Ursula said, I am glad to hear it. The words passed were sincere and that made them worse, that's what barbed them. She touched Annette's arm, regarded her for a moment longer, and then she moved on. Ushering all noise along with her. Annette gripped the trolley. Her throat glued itself shut.

Inward, she saw the true gulf between her and Frank.

She decided then what truth to believe. Love was not to be spat out when it grew mean, she reasoned, that's when you've got to scrap and bite and kick to keep hold of it. To maintain it. She chose to believe Frank and the something that they had together. Love at first touch. And she drove to the garage and asked him to swear, again and again and again, that it was only a kiss. One drunken kiss. That was all.

She watched Polly wipe the countertop. Dragging the paper in tight circles. Soaking away the wine but leaving smudgy, greasy marks. She wanted to reveal everything. Tell Polly about all of Frank's faults and failures: his uncanny ability to forget every single anniversary and birthday, tell her of the time he passed out at her sister's wedding, of his fear of rats. But also tell her of his kindnesses; the newspaper wrapped in a plastic bag in the morning before work, how he makes her feel when he wants her, the laughs, the way he and the boys playfight in the living room. Her runny eyes followed after Polly as she discarded the soiled paper into the fire.

'Actually, it's good that the boys are gone,' Polly said. She stepped forward from the fireplace. 'I wanted to show you something. I need your professional opinion.' Polly smoothed down her top, waited a second, and then pulled it up. Revealing plump breasts and a black bra with a small maroon bow at its centre and a webby design around each cup. 'Do you think he'd like this? I have others. But this one sort of sprang out at me this morning.'

'He'll like it, won't he?' Polly asked again.

'Oh,' Annette said. She clenched her stomach. 'He'll love it.'

Polly nodded, exhaled, finally shrugged down her top. Mouthed, Thank you. Annette had the notion that maybe she was expected to show her bra now. Tit for tat. But she resisted and gazed at the wine, its ripples, feeling her cheek blister.

Sitting once more, Polly hummed to herself before saying, 'You do need the couple of drinks the first time. It was the same with myself and Des. Makes it less, I don't know, stuffy. Is that the right word? But we're getting on so well, aren't we?' Polly slipped off her flats. With her middle finger, Polly picked lightly at her forehead – the very centre – and spoke again, 'He's a big man, your Frank. He's built like a bear or something. I know that's silly. But he's really boyish too, in a sort of crude way.' She rested her chin on her palm and turned to Annette. 'You're excited, aren't you?'

Annette heard the clatter of the back door. She held the stem of the glass between her fingers, deliberately, and answered, Yes, of course. She was excited.

'Did you miss us?' Desmond had a whiskey bottle. His face was redder, he had ditched the glasses. He laughed, seemed keen to emphasise his own laughter.

Frank threw himself into the far chair. His breathing was a little haggard. Off him she smelled the wind and smoke and the clean frost that must be brittle by now, that would crunch mechanically underfoot.

Frank raised his chin at her. Rubbed his face then.

Desmond switched off the telly and Polly scooched to allow him to sit in the middle of the couch.

His hand was ice on her knee.

'Wait.' Annette was surprised by her own voice. 'Wait.' By the sureness of it. 'We never got to tell you about how me and Frank met? Earlier?' Polly pulled an encouraging face, pursed her lips.

'Did we?' Annette pushed down the hem of her dress, looked at Frank.

Desmond poured some whiskey into his wine glass.

'Do you remember, Frank?' Annette said. He creased his forehead. 'Well, it was in Galway. You remember that much, surely?'

'I do,' Frank said. 'Are you feeling alright, love?'

'Do you want some water?' Polly asked.

'No, I'm fine.' Her voice was shaky for a moment, a radio marooned in static. She tucked a strand of hair behind her ear. 'We were both in Galway. That's right. I had started in a property management company and I was living by the docks. My first taste of the real world. It was a Friday and a couple of us decided to go for drinks.' She sat forward. Eyes focused on the fire, its last licks. 'It was a boring night. You know how you can never talk about anything but the job when you're out with the work crowd? But then I noticed this lump at the bar.'

Polly let out a cackle.

'Did you know even then?' Desmond laughed. His gaze was watery.

'Somehow I think I did,' she paused, considered. 'You should have seen the state of him though. A shirt that didn't fit him, these baggy boot-cut jeans. But there was something in that I liked.'

'Where you going with this, Annette?' Frank said.

'I'm telling them how we met.' She smiled at him. There was no going back. 'Why don't you explain why you were in Galway?'

He studied her, his mouth open, tongue moving. 'I was down working in a garage in Bohermore.' He spoke slowly.

'That's right. Well done,' she said. 'We got talking anyway, me and Frank. Well, I got talking to him. He was a shy lad, you see. All tongue-tied around women – if you can believe that one.' Polly squeaked. 'I kept at him, trying to get him to open up, to talk, even if I thought it was only for a laugh at first. Something to keep me from lease agreements. I remember his accent was tough as anything, like he bit into the words. But soon he started giving as good back and before I realised what was happening, I was holding his hand under the table.'

'That's sweet,' Polly said. 'Isn't it, Des?'

'I'm not finished.' Annette took a deep breath. 'What happened next, Frank?'

'Annette,' he said. 'Look, will we go home?'

She turned to him. 'What happened next?'

He cleared his throat. 'We kissed.'

Desmond offered the whiskey to Frank, who swirled it and tanked some. He roughly stroked under his jaw with his knuckles. In his own proud manner he was begging. But they had come too far. Already too much had been said. 'We kissed,' he repeated.

'We kissed and then what happened?' she asked flatly.

'Annette, for fuck sake.'

'What happened next, Frank?'

'We went back.' He held the bottle in front of him like a prop. 'The pair of us.'

'To where?'

'My digs.' He shook his head. 'Out in Shantalla.'

'And what happened?'

'You stayed over,' Frank said. 'You stayed over. And I had to kick the other bollox out of the room so that we got some sort of privacy. You stayed over. And about halfway through your man knocked on the door. Looking for his glasses. That's what happened next.'

She closed her eyes. 'And were you a virgin?'

'Oh, Christ,' Frank gasped. 'Annette, please. Will we just go?'

'Were you?' she said.

'Yes,' he shouted, 'yes, I was.'

She started to laugh. Polly nervously joined in. 'It was love,' Annette said. 'Love at first touch.' She tipped the rest of the wine into her mouth. Tasted nothing. 'What do you think?' she said, laughing still. 'Real romantic, no?' Frank slugged his whiskey when she caught his eye. She was excited. She grabbed Desmond's arm, 'Can you remind me where the bathroom is?'

She twisted on the hot water. She hadn't been this drunk in years. She bowled water in her hand till it began to prickle her skin. Then she let it collapse. She hit the other tap and wrapped her lips around it. She let the water fill her gums and spat it out in shoots. Then she dropped onto the toilet.

Her head was pounding. Her breath was laboured. Rasping. She thumbed down her underwear. Feeling the elastic pang into a slacker shape. Despite all of Frank's faults, and by Christ there were many, she knew that she loved their life. Knew that she loved him and the boys and their life. It was their life. She pressed her forehead into her palms. Her heels slid before her on the tiles. Him and the boys were her life and she needed only reassurance. She needed only to let the venom dull a little. It will make them stronger, tonight. Make them even.

The black lace thong, stringed with tiffany flowers, was stretched between her ankles. It had cost her forty euro. Meant to arouse. Show who was in control. She rose from the toilet, steadying herself on the sink. What had kept her going? With her heel, she pared her left leg from the thong and shook it altogether off the right. Does it get easier? Vapour had fogged the oval mirror, and she studied her reflection as if watching a woman across the street: the woman who was carrying too much shopping, the woman who was younger, the woman who resembled an old acquaintance. Annette picked the underwear off the tiled floor. She looked at herself, the balled thong, and threw it into the toilet.

The Gallaghers were huddled on the couch. Frank was in his chair. Talk ceased as she entered the room. The candles had run down, corkscrew smoke swirled from their tips. The curtain had been messed with again, the right cloth not quite centre. Between this gap, she saw how the frost had settled hard on the front garden. This expanse of white.

'How you feeling, love?' Frank stuttered to his feet. She went to him, held his hand, and kissed him – his tongue nettley and unaware. She felt for the pulse in his jeans. She took it, groped it, and with her other hand light on his shoulders, shoved him back into his chair. 'Love?' he blinked up at her. She roped her hand around Polly's elbow and led her to Frank's lap. Polly giggled.

Annette tucked herself in beside Desmond. He grinned. With the ball of his thumb, he strummed her upper arm. She looked again at the print on the wall, the one of the couple in the brown field. A basket was by her feet as she prayed, a pitchfork by his as he wrung his cap.

Desmond's fingers skimmed along her shoulder and slipped under the strap of her dress. 'You're feeling better?' The strap fell from her shoulder. He was enjoying this, she could tell. 'I thought I lost you.'

He positioned her hand on his leg.

Her eyes darted once as fingers treaded further along her back.

'You're not nervous?' he spoke into her ear. The words warm, clammy.

'No,' she said, 'I'm not nervous at all.'

# Howya, Horse

When the horse with the lurcher face barged through the front door of the mansion on the hill, thunderously, jarringly, horsily, Cotter was explaining to Marian that it was *actually* no huge deal for him to have cummed inside her, and though he should not have done it in the first place, because A, she had explicitly warned him not to as she hated the idea, because B, he had promised he'd hundred percent not cum inside her as she hated the idea, the fact of the matter was that a rubber johnny had been snugly and securely wrapped upon him, that the heated juice was consequently swaddled up inside it, and, therefore, aside from her own icky superstition, how bad, really and truly? They were on the landing of an L-shaped staircase, overlooking an expansive living room. Both were a little sweaty. Both hastily dressed. Cotter's explanation was not going down brilliantly, though he was unsure why he required it to go down brilliantly at all. And so when this new steedy intruder to the houseparty skidded into the living room – the breaking-screech of horseshoe encountering varnished floor, the bump and scamper of its ungainly motion – he was more than happy to interrupt himself mid-line with a dreamy mutter of, Watch the horsey, as the animal's vein-knotted rump knocked the flat-screen television and clattered into the bookshelves spanning the far wall.

There was a gasp from below; someone sprang for cover behind the couch; someone let drop a beerbottle. A tall, skinny lamp tumbled over. The bulb flickered and then went completely. The horse shook its head, stamped on the floorplanks and let out a kind of quivering vroom. Was it hurt? Was it dazed? Now the only light in the room was from a laptop braced on the arm of the couch, which presently went flying as the horse swung around and became entangled in the laptop's charger. Glass appeared on the rug like fresh crusty snow. Music and light vanished as the laptop hit the stone fireplace. On a leather recliner, a dozy Boner suddenly yanked back the footrest to make way for the horse. The three other bucks in the room flattened themselves against the wall. Cotter went to hold Mar's hand and she snapped it from him. Don't you dare, she said flatly. The horse had a cream mane, a freckled belly, and this haggard white coat that resembled more Tipp-Ex scrawled across page than downy rabbittail white. From the hallway, there was a clucking intake of breath and a single loud scream. Then there was more.

Cotter and Marian watched, marvelled, as the horse manoeuvred through the living room into the adjacent dining area – hoofs plinking on clay-coloured tile. A humid stank wafted: perspiring horse and the fug of shit and the outside. A face loomed over the banister and asked, What the hell is after happening? Cotter pointed down as if obvious. He said, A horse. There was a meaty thud from the dining room, and subsequent hurried, scratchy noises. In one action, Boner scrambled up from the recliner and gathered his Buckfast under his arm, then he flopped over the fallen TV. Liquid gushed from his bottle. A voice inexplicably roared, Fire, fire. One by one the main lights were switched on, and Cotter had to blink rapidly against their lurid glare before he noticed Tara, their host, had stumbled into the living room. The back of her white jeans and lacy croptop were caked in muck and grass. Her nose was crooked, piddling red.

What is she at? he heard Marian whisper.

It was about one at night. It was early May and now it was Sunday. They were down the stairs when they saw the horse kick out and clip the chandelier and a hefty lad being caught by a hoof on the follow through. A sickening crack. The buck yelped, crumbled, fondled his jaw in a ball on the floor. The pop of a bottle hitting a wall; this was repeated. Two girls raced by them up the stairs. Tara dragged her left leg and cooed, Dorrie, no, no. A can of Dutch Gold was hopped against the horse's burly neck. More screams. The sound of doors slamming. The horse reared up again. Marian murmured about the absolute state of this, and Cotter wasn't totally sure if she meant the horse, or the houseparty, or maybe just the Island in general. He turned and examined her face – her bug eyes ringed with mascara, her irises the loveliest poo-brown of stretched caramel; her arms were crossed and her boy-hair was tousled; her cheeks were marginally flushed and he wondered should he not touch them to reassure her he'd protect her from the rampaging horse and to check if she had forgotten about her fury re the cum – and then Marian stepped forward, was stood in front of him, and, meeting his wistful gaze, she ordered Cotter to fuck off forever from her life.

Without another word, Marian strode through the living room and into the hallway. Cotter called, then quickly followed. There were photographs of Tara, and her sister Molly, and the little brother, and Molly riding many different horses all strewn about the hallway floor, like a card trick gone wrong. Cotter was shoeless, sported only plain white ankle socks, and so he treaded on his tippy toes to dodge the powder and crumbs from these photo frames. The front door was wide open. It wasn't deliberate, you know, Cotter went on. I tried to stop, like. Wait, Mar. Listen to me.

Look, if anything, he said to her with a foot on the front step, it's a massive compliment to you. Cotter struck a cheeky pose at this remark: tongue swabbing his upper lip, one leg a little stuck out. It was a bold move, attempting a joke now, but one he believed could sway her, as it was so untimely that it would suit her bleak sense of humour, so inopportune that she'd have to succumb to its charm, and then it was apparent to him, standing there with his arms akimbo and a dumb simper on his face, that it was the wrong move to make, it was the wrongest move. Instead of the gag being received with anger or amusement from Marian, some frisson of reaction which Cotter could bend and use for his own benefit, it was met with uninterest, with silence.

Cotter shouted her name, continuing after her.

There was a terrific wail from the kitchen. The sound of plates and cups being dropped. Followed by the bigger sound of a horse in a kitchen.

I love you, he told Marian. She was headed around the back of the mansion. There were potted plants and a wheeled barbecue. Stone patio. Cigarette butts like lice. Clearing his throat, Cotter tried to come up with something better to say, a more decisive statement that would surely split Marian's heart and allow him to fester within it. He could mention how they were sort of together six months, but didn't it mean so much longer? Or guilt her, remind her how he got the bus down to Westport for her portfolio-fashion-show-thing, had stayed for almost an hour? He combed a hank of hair behind his ear. Don't you know I love you? he said to her once more.

There was a cackle to this.

Then she announced, You're a bad liar.

At the fuzzy line between the blued darkness of the outside and the amber glaze offered by the porch lights, she waited for him, and when he edged near, she shook her head slowly, looked up at the house and its bright yellow windows, before saying: Get away from my life, Cotter. I'm sick of it. No, don't come any closer. On the last stressed word, she released a breath and it rose above her in a tangerine cloud. There was a twitchy crease over her right brow but aside from that, her expression was one of steady composure, which made this all the more alarming to Cotter. And she wasn't crying, nor was there a hint of soon-to-rain tears, which surprised him, though he did not wish to admit to this surprise. For to admit such a thing meant to sort of want it to have happened. It would suggest he was a bad person, and, importantly, he was not the bad one here.

I've tried really hard, she said then, and it felt like something private that Cotter should not be able to hear.

She looked at him, and her eyes were shiny. Stay away from me.

To this, Cotter didn't know what to say, and he shrugged feebly, and lifted his arms in proposal for a hug, a cuddle, and, in response, Marian raised her voice for the first time: Stay the fuck away.

She began to march down the sharply sloped garden. Almost immediately, he lost her in the darkness, could not distinguish her lanky poolcue frame amidst the silky blues and indigoes and violets of summerish nighttime, and he thought to roar for her to stall, to be careful – he knew there was a dog somewhere, and maybe more wild horses? – when the slit of her figure was suddenly aglow, formed by what must have been the flashlight from her phone. Cotter had an airy, open sensation in his gut, like he had been kidney-shotted. It felt like defeat. Except hadn't he won?

Will you cop on, Marian, Cotter yelled into the blue.

He could just leave things as they were now. Let her off alone. And let himself rejoin the party alone. Whatever was between them was done, or at least Cotter's role in it was done for the next while. Plus, if anyone was to chase anyone it should be her. It should be her pursuing him, all weighed down and gross with guilt. He was in the correct. She was wrong. Cotter reminded himself not to forget this fact.

But he did love her. That wasn't a lie. He loved her in the only way you can love your first proper girlfriend: sporadically.

And, also, he didn't think he was a bad liar.

From inside the mansion came a smash, accompanied by a deranged howl. Cotter turned and saw a crowd at the rear sliding door, someone was being carried out and he recognised none of these faces, all unfamiliar, and he figured they must be Tara's pals from college with their polite, gammy accents and coloured chinos, and all at once this crowd spun and scattered in different directions – some collapsing outside, others disappearing deeper into the mansion. A glimpse of the horse through the sliding door. The fella who was being carried now pulled himself along the patio and into the soil beneath a rose bush, where he started to sob. Amidst this racket, Cotter thought he could vaguely hear Tara pleading to the horse: Dorrie, will you not chill?

Then Boner reversed out the sliding door. His lumberjack shirt was unbuttoned and flapped and revealed a grey tee with an image of Mr Lazy on it. Cotter had once considered Boner the best friend. What the F, Boner wheezed, and he clocked Cotter's presence at the end of the patio. Man, he said, breathless, wandering over. Did you see the horse? What the F, like.

Cotter answered that he had, obviously, and was so irritated by the simplicity of this question he felt provoked to mock it. It's a horse inside a house, Boner, he said, how could you possibly not see it?

Exactly, Boner replied, nodding. He was wide-eyed, pink-eyed. Plainly still whacked.

Facing the garden again, Cotter heard himself say, It looks like a lurcher. The horse. The face of it does.

A what? Boner was patting the many pockets of his combat pants.

A lurcher, Cotter said and said it again, annoyed to have spoken at all. He hesitated a sock onto the grass, searched for and found the glint of silver gliding down the garden like a knife repeatedly flashed. She hadn't ventured too far ahead yet. Frowning, Cotter ground together his molars – a delicate icy pain – and he informed himself he should not do what he knew he was about to do. But before he could step off the patio and chase, he had to first clarify: It's a breed of dog, Boner. The lurcher. Skinny yokes. You'd know it to see, like.

Ah, Boner answered. Then he said, Not a clue, sorry.

The ground sank beneath Cotter though he reassured himself that he was not running but rather walking speedily after her. His socks were sopping. Shoes, jacket, phone, all upstairs. In his mouth, a leathery taste that he associated with fucking a situation spectacularly up – he recalled last December, the unvented hall in the leisure centre, the chair with the creaking steel back, the row upon row of bowed heads, and the taste crisping his mouth as he scanned through the exam paper and discovered that he comprehended absolutely diddley-squat and that after a single measly semester, college, for him, was over.

To his right, a spaniel was tied to a shed by its lead.

There was the circle of deckchairs where he and Boner had chatted earlier.

Cotter trod on something mushy and tried not to guess what it was.

It was cloudless and, naturally, overhead stars were splattered at random, like gravel tacked to a grazed bloody knee. The moon hung to his left. The frost shone damp and offered a rainbow tint to the grass as he narrowed his stare to her descending figure in the distance. He had learned from Marian that this garden eventually smoothed out to where there were fields for the horses, a massive stable, and even a racing track.

He called to her, Where you going, Mar?

He cursed and called again, I'm coming like, will you hold on.

Slowing, Marian approached a chunky galvanised gate, eerily unlocked, the dimensions of its meshed bars foggy against the surrounding blue, and it was the kind of spot where Cotter presumed she'd come to a halt upon hearing he was near, they'd both come to a halt, where she might freak at him in privacy, where she'd recite past offenses between gulps of air, or maybe she'd gently ask him to locate Tara for her; Tara the pal who'd innately understand and balm all, it was the kind of spot where they'd likely reconcile if they were to reconcile tonight, where she'd apologise if she was to apologise tonight, and at this gate, Marian kept on walking. There wasn't a flick of neck, a glance to confirm he was trailing her. She just kept walking.

It shocked Cotter, and he roared her name.

And Marian took the time to bolt the gate after her, untroubled.

The light from her phone was growing dimmer and dimmer, and Cotter watched as it blew away completely once Marian clambered over some obstacle at the opposite end of the field. The smell of cigarettes in the breeze, the honey of blossomed gorse. The shadows of horses snorting, shuffling. If Cotter held his breath here, inhaled as if to sing choirly, he sensed he might be able to hear Mar's breath ways across the fields and, undoubtedly, he told himself, it would be bleating with high, torrid emotion as she trudged further on, further from him. But he didn't test this.

He supposed she was heading for home, though her home was a fair whack away. It was probably dangerous for her to undertake such a trek, what with rapists, horny drunks, her gloomy clothing, unlit backroads, etc., but what could Cotter do? Apart from catching up with Marian and escorting her until she arrived home. But why should he do that? She had walked off on him. It was her choice and he had followed her loyally and she had kept going without a care for him and would she do the same if the roles were swapped? Facts were pivoting and in this fresh slant, Cotter was the noble victim once more. Yes, it'd be her own fault if something awful was to occur. And honestly, he'd have zero sympathy if anything terrible did happen on her sulk home because it was her own fault.

Then Cotter felt horrible and reworked this opinion: he'd have sympathy if anything bad did befall her, of course, yes, but he'd reserve the right to have an I-told-you-so attitude about whatever the bad may be. This seemed more than fair.

And with a start, Cotter realised he still wore the condom.

He reached down and confirmed, a slick and gooey confirmation, and he carefully unfurled it. In his palm, withered as a mishandled strip of Sellotape, the tube was coarser, more adhesive, like a cat's tongue. The pinpricked holes were small humps when he so brushed his thumb back and forth.

Eventually, he tossed the condom.

Behind him low indistinct voices swarmed and now and again a full word burst forward intelligibly to his ears like fireworks. The party had adapted to the outside and Cotter could not face it yet. He wiggled and cracked the joints on his fingers, relishing the bony clicks. Then he went out of his way to kick the gate, and it hurt his big toe. An urge to pelt after her coursed through him, wouldn't burn out, and Cotter tried to distract himself from it by planning his week ahead – his father had imparted this stress-relieving strategy to Cotter upon his third week of college, when

Cotter was already drowning, when he rang home and was unable to hold the phone still – and so Cotter reflected on how he had work tomorrow evening in The Island Head, then a split shift Tuesday, and the same Wednesday, and thankfully just morning Thursday, and he had to pause here because his mind started to whirl and scream. He squatted down and held his face with both hands. Without wanting to, he envisioned his mother ironing his shirt and black slacks and waistcoat tomorrow afternoon. Then he saw his father driving him over to the hotel and being parked around the side when Cotter punched off – the newspaper spread on the steering wheel so that Cotter would only be able to make out his father's neat greying combover. These were events already in existence, Cotter felt now, events already spinning. They had happened, were happening, will happen endlessly. They were like the glitter of stars at night. The roll of sea. Unavoidable. Indelible.

Marian was leaving in two weeks. Well, less now.

She was going to stay with a cousin at first. Find a job. Get a headstart on college work. She had explained all this to him one afternoon, giddy. They were meant to be watching a film. So that was annoying, in and of itself. He had listened to her and nodded, tried to smile normally, but the fervour of her words mocked him.

He looked up at the dark blue sky and then back down at the trampled muck. He rested his hands between his thighs. Everything was suddenly going too fast.

What was he at with his own life? What was there to look forward to?

Cotter shut his eyes and his mouth sort of hummed and he kept his eyes closed.

Fuck you, Marian, he said, and it came out much louder than he had expected it to. Fuck you and just leave. I don't fuckin give a shit. I don't care about you. You're a fuckin bitch. You're a cunt. You hear me. You're a fucking cunt. I don't care about you, I never did.

For a while Cotter stayed by the gate, lips moving and widening as if he were still howling, and then he rose and wiped his face and began the hike back up to the party. By now his feet were numb, the socks soaked through. His hands glowed with the cold. In his mind, he went over his story, practised certain sections aloud, washing the finer details until they were clean and straight. How she was mental and a looper and needed to get her head properly checked. How he had worn a johnny, so what was the huge deal? What was the fuss? How she had stormed off. Yes, he had smashed up whatever they were. Yes, he had discarded her. He didn't want to move to London, actually. No interest. Zero interest. She begged and begged for him to accompany her, but he chose not to because, as he said, she was honestly completely mental, and he had zero interest.

A few from the party had arranged themselves on the grass, sharing cans and Tayto with their backs to the mansion, but the majority were congested on the patio. The dog was unleashed and surrounded by a mob, who scraped the delirious fella's exposed belly. All the windows were bright yellow. A girl was spread out flat on the patio and another girl, named Sarah something or other, kneeled beside her, stroking the prone girl's hand. Sarah rolled her eyes when Cotter caught her blank stare. On his hunkers, Boner was lurking behind these two, the neck of a Mexican beerbottle dangling between his fingers. He shouted to Cotter, You meant a greyhound, earlier. Then he said, Where's your shoes? On the second floor, a window had been broken and the path beneath was drizzled in glass, like hedge cuttings. A runnel of steamy puke oozed beside a drain. There was another bronze pool of sick or beer. In the air, the smell of spilt vodka and weed and sweat saturated within the folds of clothing. A crew were posing peacefully for a phone. The rear sliding door was shut, and Tara was crouched before it with her head cradled in her hands, rocking. There was loud speculation of more wine stashed in the shed. A slobbery couple were coiled on the window ledge, people were clustered very close together and talking loudly and emptily. And only when he reached the sticky middle of these collected bodies, registered paled faces he had seen earlier when not pale, heard weeping and croaky demands for Guards or firefighters or a humble vet, listened to an igniting quarrel between two boys over the ownership of a deckchair, did Cotter recall that there was a horse inside the house.

I'm about to puke, Tara declared with real confidence. Her arse was pressed against the shower's frosted doors, which rasped and shifted from this pressure, and she was stooped forward as if about to dive into a pool. The bathroom appeared to her in shades of charcoal and slate and wet stone.

You're not, Marian replied.

I am, Tara said, I really am. She lost her footing, jutted forward, and regained her balance with a frantic wave of arm. Ow, she cried, and she was aware she was acting like a small child but it was a small child who was seriously ill. She propped a shoulder against the shower, allowed her head to fall back. Honestly, Marian, Tara said.

From the toilet, Marian eyed her coldly. Well, if you are, do it in the sink.

Obeying, Tara waddled towards the basin embedded in a black granite square. A toothbrush dropped to the floor, her own actually, and a plastic cup as her elbows plonked themselves over the taps. Tara coughed and began to retch, and her shoulders bucked up and down, but only pulpy strings of saliva spilled from her mouth, congealing before the drain like a yolkless egg.

Tara whimpered.

What did I tell you? Marian said, and they exchanged a glance.

Tara said, You lousy bitch, and Marian laughed hard.

Pushing against the countertop of the sink, Tara tried and promptly failed to straighten herself up, and so instead Tara chose to plunge her shoulders and every-thing above her shoulders inside the wide basin. Marian cackled. In the sink, Tara pouted and craned her neck as best she could to scrutinise her reflection in the mirror. Her foundation was dusty, particularly along her nose, unveiling her rotten freckles. Her hair was no longer in a cute bun but was an unruly hillock at her crown. And she wore gigantic dish-framed sunglasses that belonged to her sister, Molly. They were expensive, and she wondered had she nabbed them from Molly's room as a joke? She could sort of pinpoint the humour in such a stunt, could sort of visualise herself mimicking Molly to applause. Then Tara felt a sudden reduction in her stomach. A flattening, like dough being mushed over and over by rolling pin.

She rotated her head and gagged and gagged and, briefly, she felt that the badness inside her was about to be released, and then nothing substantial spewed from her mouth but more of this bubbling saliva.

Her stomach continued to rumble though, and as Tara tilted her head in the basin to better complain to Marian, her stomach seemed to flip itself over entirely, a new stabbing pain, and desperate now, desperately, Tara gunned two fingers and shoved them into her mouth.

There was a robust surge from the bottom of her throat, as if a pinball had been dislodged, and before Tara could ready herself, she had vomited a rope of liquid.

Tara blinked and then there was a heap of the stuff in the sink, glistening. A reek of alcohol and vinegar. She shivered, she swept strings of hair from her lips.

Oh, Jesus, Marian said, rising from the toilet. Crabwalking from the jeans stretched below her knees, Marian handed Tara a towel, who grabbed it and put it on her head as a pretty wedding veil. The toilet flushed and after a moment, Marian sighed and snatched the towel and started to wipe Tara's mouth.

What did you take? Marian asked and kept muttering Jesus and God like she was conducting a prayer.

Marian, Tara cried. I'm really, really sick.

I know, girl, Marian said, I know. The towelling ceased and she began to rub Tara's back, which was so nice and kind, and then Tara felt her left arm being taken, not quite firmly, and turned to the underside. Marian asked with unsettling softness: When did this happen?

There was a knock on the door, a cautious test of the handle. Marian shouted for them to use the bathroom downstairs. Tara gazed into the mirror. Marian was bent over her, studying Tara's arm as if certain to read significance in the ridged cuts along her wrist. Marian had shaved her hair very short and you know, it wasn't for Tara, but go Marian all the same. Go get it, hun, Tara thought.

Tara. Marian's voice was softer, scarier. When?

I love you, Tara said to the mirror. I love you so much. And your hair, too.

Answer me.

Don't be mean, Tara said. Please, be nice to me. Then Tara shuddered and puked again.

Marian backed from her. The arm was let go.

Another rap on the door. Are you deaf? Marian hissed at it.

It's me, the door said.

Tara recognised the voice. Moany like an electric razor. What does he want now? she said to Marian. Tell him to go away, Marian. With her elbows, Tara lifted herself up from the basin and yelled for the door to go away.

Marian shushed her.

Marian said to the door, One second, alright? She bit her lower lip, in the mirror Tara saw this.

I have to talk to him, Marian said closer to Tara's ear. You're alright now, aren't you? Here, hold on. Marian guided Tara's face to running water, which Tara duly drank and dribbled, which tasted like chicken from the fridge.

The door knocked again.

Give me a second, Cotter, Marian shouted.

Under her breath, Tara said, Yeah, Fuckface. She had stopped drinking the water, but Marian's hold was unaltered.

Heya, Tara whispered at last, and Marian replied as if she was the one who spoke first: I have to talk to him, I think. Just, I think I should talk to him. You understand, don't you?

In the mirror, Tara watched Marian flip off the tap. Then Tara blinked and the room swayed and there was colour and she fixed her glasses and now she watched Marian examining herself in the mirror, cocking her chin slightly, pulling out sections of her woolly poloneck. Marian was beautiful. You'll be alright, Marian said, you're fine, really.

Marian added: And we'll talk about the other thing tomorrow. OK? Promise me?

Tara watched herself nod and nod and nod.

Then in the mirror it was only Tara with an empty tub behind her – the towel stained from her vomit drooping like eviscerated guts. The door was ajar. Echoes from the party drifted in. Shrill babble. Very loud rap music. Her toothbrush and the plastic cup were returned to the sink. She still had on Molly's dumb sunglasses. Flecked around her chin were what she decided were oats, porridge oats, and so how could it be revolting that she was scrubbing them off with the heel of her hand?

Tara was outside, staggering down the back garden. She had no notion where she was heading, but that was fine. Above, the stars were dwindling and brightening like someone was toggling the dimmer switch. She was arrowing through gravel and now back onto grass and weaving towards the bluest darkness. Here was a procession of people she knew, drinking in a square, smoke billowing like speech bubbles, friends she had invited to her home on the Island, and she hated them. Something was called and she guessed this was called at her and immediately, Tara shot the finger back at whoever wanted her attention. Throaty laughter. Someone cawed, She's done you, bud. I must go tend to the crops, Tara squealed in a Brit accent. Tara laughed at her own joke. It was hilarious. She was hilarious. She took a swig from the can which she discovered she was carrying.

She was braced against the gate for the horses, her forehead lolling on the topmost bar. Despite the shakiness of her arms, it was not that cold out. She no longer possessed Molly's sunglasses – no idea when they had been discarded. The can had been chucked into a bush. Tara desired to theatrically shriek into the darkness, fill the darkness, but she had thus far resisted. She knew she should not do this while the party was ongoing. The disruptor, the creator of the scene that prematurely ended the houseparty, was not going to be Tara tonight. Sugary cider lingered in her mouth, and her front teeth were still coated in vomit – a vinegary shock when her tongue swam in a certain way. She blamed her unwellness entirely on Boner: she had scrimped a wee bump from him earlier which had shot her way, way west.

Gulping, Tara notified herself not to talk to him ever again.

The five horses were clustered together – without opening her eyes she would have been able to confirm they were nearby from that mulchy stench – and they were oddly quiet. Well, wankers, Tara said to them in greeting. She had never got the appeal of horses. Her father adored them – since he had sold his fish farming business, they had become his only chance to fail – hence Tara had been practically reared astride them. And despite the lessons, the daytrips to races in polkadot dresses, the glam shows, the galloping, the pageants, the shined stirrups, the feathery ribbon pinned to her chest for leaping an animal over a knee-high pole when she was eight years old, she held no profound or nostalgic affection for them: they were grand, she didn't want them to die or anything. Molly adored them though, and Tara often wondered did her father change his approach the second time round. And would Timmy come to love them as well? Tara's mother was as detached from the horses as Tara was – a browning image of her mother smoking in the car as the rest of them watched lustrous horse after lustrous horse loop a sandy track on an overcast Sunday.

But her mother was basically disinterested in life.

Tara did not like her mother. Or her father, to be fair.

A horse roamed from the group. A sound like thick hair being brushed through.

In Tara's pocket, her phone rang and was unanswered.

She did not like most of those attending her party either, if she was honest and, presently, she was incredibly honest. She was obligated to invite half of them due to the smallness of her course, and more than half of them had driven down and were bunking in the house tonight, their rolled sleeping bags piled in the utility room like a decayed honeycomb. She liked only pieces of college, and she didn't like Dublin at all, and Marian could be ridiculously selfish, could be such a hypocrite, and her new haircut was an horrendous idea, and she didn't like Molly most of the time, and Timmy was practically a baby, and she hated her parents, and she hated these stinking horses, and she especially hated herself.

She wondered was it a shit party? Were they all having a shit time? If so, good.

She wondered if Marian and Cotter were arguing, if they were ending? If so, good.

You know what? She should scream and freak at all those inside her house. It was her party. She should go freak at Marian, too. Then she should hit Cotter repeatedly with a brush or something. She should run everyone from her house. She should cause the scene. She should unplug the party. It was hers to ruin, so why not ruin it?

She took a deep breath.

This fantasy, Tara knew, was classic Tara. She was always the mess, and, apparently, wanted to be the mess.

The lone horse wandered over and nudged her elbow with its muzzle. Expecting grub, Tara figured. I don't have anything, you fool, she explained to the horse, and her voice sounded wobbly. She used to feed the horses after school. It had been her one chore. They were greedy fuckers, she remembered. They'd scoot over to the gate before she was even halfway down the garden. Take the fingers off you if you weren't quick. Ugly eaters, too. Loud. Grubby pianokey teeth. Was this a good or a bad memory? She didn't know. She regarded the horse now, and, after a moment, stroked it, softly, mumbling, softly, Who is the best boy? Its coat was rough against her fingertips like blistered paint on a wall. She recalled the horse's name and sang it – Dorrie, Dorrie – and patting it, corrected herself, Who is the best girl? And recalling her old chore and the horse's name and her parents and her perfect sister and the party raging beyond and, finally, her own self, Tara unhurriedly drew back her neck and walloped the animal very hard with her forehead.

The horse thrashed away. It let out a whistled snort and Tara understood the pain in it as the headbutt sent her angelically backwards. A flash of light split her vision and the night sky was dappled with dizzying rosegold. Her nose was bleeding profusely. She yanked at the grass about her. Her chunky runners worked into the muck, before she curled into herself, arms around her shoulders. She licked and drank the red as it streamed warmly from her nose.

She sensed a new freedom, sprawled there in the dirt, a room previously locked. She had done something spontaneous and violent, she had clasped the reins of her life and swerved it off course, she had headbutted the steed hellbent on delivering her to mediocrity, boringness. It was control. It was delicious. In a nostril – the still functioning left nostril – the smell of a burnt out fuse. Her breath sparkled, a mist, and she beamed at it. She was aware she was awfully drunk, but that didn't negate this newfound freedom, this unlocking. Why should it? With her tongue, she probed her front tooth and it moved easily.

The gate rattled and rattled louder, and with difficulty, Tara peeked over. The horse was banging into the gate and now into the other horses. She shook herself, tried to awake to the reality of the situation. The world was spinning. Her crushed nose appeared as a fin to her right eye. She began to negotiate with herself: Stand up, say you're sorry to Dorrie, and afterward you can lie here all night long.

These were tense and arduous negotiations.

She managed to get to her knees and grabble forward till a hand found the stiff handle of the gate. Then grappling the bars, she stood. Or not quite stood, but leaned. She was groggy. Against the blue night sky, the stars were falling dangerously. I'm sorry, she said, Dorrie, I'm very sorry about that. Towards the horse, she felt sorrow and immense empathy. In a manner of speaking, she too had been headbutted, she thought wisely, but in her case it was by life. She jemmied open the gate. Dorrie, she whispered, I really am sorry. Wading toward the spooked horse, she asked, Who's the best girl? And the horse knocked her sideways, a tumultuous force, a lung-emptying force, and a hoof landed on her thigh. Tara screamed, she recoiled, and held the leg with both hands. She couldn't breathe, she could not breathe, and then she could, but only barely. Rolling onto her side, huffing out roasted air, she watched in agony as the horse raced for the house. Its coat becoming clearer and clearer, whiter and whiter.

Fuck, Tara said to herself. Oh, fuck.

All at once the frequency of Cotter's voice seemed off to Marian. Sullen and sort of nervy and deepening as he asked, Will I fetch a condom? Also, his use of that strange word, *fetch*. And the way he jolted back from her in the bed, clumsily unlacing his fingers from hers. Yet earlier, after brief turmoil outside the bathroom, they had joked and yapped and kissed and grubbed at what was inside one another's jeans, and that had all rung to Marian as normal, his wording normal, his fondling behaviour normal. But now, as she watched him climb from the bed, tugging at his polo shirt to cover his ass, she was certain there was something altogether off with him. From this new perspective, other events in the day reshaped themselves: Why had he been snubbing her texts and calls unless he was crabbed? Why had he come to the party late and not really drinking and searched for her only after hanging outside with Matthew Comer, who, Cotter had frequently informed her, was literally a corpse to him? She was naked from the waist down. She was under Buzz Lightyear bedsheets that were warm, clingy. There was an inch-wide pewter border smouldering around the curtains, glow-in-the-dark planets stickered in a pattern on the bedside wall. What's wrong with you now? Marian said.

Cotter half showed his face, a comical scowl. He gripped his cock with both hands as if only screwing it on. Nothing's wrong, he said to her. What are you on about? There was an incredulous bluff to his voice on this second utterance, a tut and then shrill finish. He turned back to the chestnut drawer, where his jacket lay. She watched his right hand oscillate, and the other hand paw at the jacket's many zips. He wore nothing but ankle socks and the grey Fred Perry shirt – the one she liked, had picked out – and his ghostly, gangly legs stood out against the room's ashen gloom. They packed no muscle, his legs, and she felt shallow any time she judged them unattractive, unmanly. In the last year, she had moulded herself into a person who was rigorously unshallow.

Marian lay back, repositioned a pillow with Woody's face on it, and stared at the ceiling. Never mind, so, she said. She scrunched her face and thought of Tara and Tara's arm and progressed to Cotter and then rewound to Tara and she couldn't let the connection slip, though she knew this particular subject was not safe or welcome territory. She began speaking: I'm worried for Tara. I don't think she likes Dublin. Well. I know for a fact she doesn't like Dublin, but I feel like she doesn't like her course. Or college, more generally. The lifestyle, I mean. She hasn't said anything to me, you know, directly, but – I don't know. I just feel she doesn't like it. And I told you before how she can get? Remember I told you? So, I'm worried. And I don't know about these new friends, either. They all seem a bit stuck up, don't they? Clueless? They don't seem to care about her.

It's tough for everybody, Cotter, she said.

Cotter agreed when it became apparent that she had left a deliberate gap.

Then he said, Tara is a weirdo, though.

Marian instructed herself not to reply immediately. She glanced over. He was still frisking his jacket. OK, she said evenly. That's not really relevant, though, is it?

The moment when she and Cotter could have talked about London had passed, a moment when she could have lied or bargained with half-lies or even been honest, and now the topic had been shelved, nice and high, and was far too easy to ignore. Anyway she felt she could plausibly guess how her moving would eventually be brought down from this lofty shelf: it would be on her first night in London, drained from the flight and finding her cousin's flat, and Cotter would text to affirm she was alive, that there had been no fiery plane crash, and then via further texts, in which his initial cheerful optimism would gradually bleed out, he would remark with astonishment about the new watery distance between them, as if it had been unexpected until then, as if London had until very recently been in the centre of Mayo, and via too many words he would explain why they might maybe now perhaps have to call it quits, sooner rather than later, on whatever they were – he'd conveniently forget they had been classified as boyfriend and girlfriend since New Year's – before it got too much for them, before the arguing and the longing and the long separation and you know yourself?, and with too few words, Marian would agree with this grim prognosis, thus sealing that they would never be civilised to one another again. This prediction didn't necessarily upset Marian, though she foresaw tears on her part because it would coincide with her being adrift from home for the first time and stress and all that dreary jazz. Rather it made her feel pity. An assumption that she'd be fine and dandy, but wasn't it sad that this boy, in the end, would not.

She flopped onto her side, reached for her phone, checked messages, thumbed an app, scrolled, then scolded herself for doing so. For avoiding the moment even if the moment was shite. She put down the phone. She could near touch the music thumping dully up through the floorboards. And there were voices singing in the hallway. She shut her eyes. Occasionally, Marian did experience doubts about leaving, prickling doubts about why she suspected she should be someone who gets to leave, why she considered her work good enough and, in turn, why she considered herself good enough, but on most of the other occasions she felt very, very justified and, frankly, desperate to be who she was going to be once over there. Tomorrow, rattled, she'd view tonight, this houseparty, this sneaky fuck, as one of those latter validating occasions. A memory she'd wield in the future, when brittle, when sore, to drive her onwards. It would act as a match. And now it became evident to her that this was to be the last time they'd have sex before she went. Her and Cotter. Without realising it, she had arrived at this conclusion and she knew it was the right one.

Ready? Cotter asked.

She laughed too loudly at this.

He was saying, I'll take that as a yes, so.

The temperature dropped as he slid under the sheets. He fidgeted. His hand was on her hip and it was like frost from his sickly circulation. Gooseflesh on her arms. A foot nudged itself between hers. A line of frost beginning at her hip. Turning, opening her eyes, she saw that he seemed to want to speak, this bewildered grimace she knew too well, and she kissed him to shut him up. The small bed was cranky as they contorted, it gave out to them, and then there was a niceness that closed her eyes again, and halfway through, she found herself wondering whether anyone could hear them, and subsequently wondering whether she'd care if anyone did hear them, whether she truly cared about what anyone else thought of her at this party, or on this craggy Island, and whether that was an egotistical or sophisticated stance to have, and whether it was perverted to be fucking in Tara's little brother's room, who she had babysat before, and then Marian was ashamed because she was no longer taking this act, this gamely hump and thrust, at all seriously, when, beneath her, Cotter whined suddenly, gratefully. She looked down at him, confused. She felt moistness under her arms, slobber on her neck and left tit. Unsticking herself from him, she watched Cotter swallow like there was a pill buried in his throat. He was blushing and he pushed his hands through his hair. A look sideways at her and there was an apology, out of nowhere, out of the muggy air, or at least she heard the word sorry gasped a couple of times, and she was propped up on her elbows, brow wrinkled, when she distinctly heard the word *cummed.*

There had been a divergence in their broad genial chatter, when or why Boner couldn't recount, but they were now rutted in opinions, and he was arguing for the existence of entrance exams for secondary schools. A topic, a supposed personal opinion, that Boner did not give a flying flip about. Cotter was against this motion, of course, that was the fun. They were outside, sitting across from one another. There were folded paper plates under their chairs, gummed with the charcoal remains of barbecued sausages. The sun was lowering to their faraway right – weak pink rippling after it and the faintest glimmer of stars, like freckles and flesh beneath a flimsy bedsheet. Boner went on, You have to be fair to the other kids, though. The smart ones. You have to crop them together cause, like, you have to inspire them. You get me? Boner paused here, noted Cotter's foot hopping up and down, noted Cotter's ballooning face as he strained to gag himself until it was his turn to speak. Boner finally said in the lightest manner to maximise the exasperation: Why should the smart ones suffer cause of the dum-dums?

That is horseshit, Cotter clasped his head with both hands and leaned back in his chair. He was so righteously furious as to be unable to fully articulate himself and he kept returning to the same hot statements of disbelief. What are you talking about? You really think that, Boner? You think that? Boner smirked and Cotter bounced from the deckchair and was suddenly standing over Boner – for a second, Boner was sure a punch was incoming and he kind of welcomed it – and then Cotter swivelled, started to walk away. That's classist, Cotter said, and he punted an empty can. That's what it is.

Boner twisted in the chair to stifle the giggles. Simon, Róisín, and this prick Jamie were nearby, sharing an emerald bottle of fizzy wine. He winked over at them. Simon gestured wankerly at Cotter, mouthed, Who's this?, and Boner winked again. Boner brought the warm can to his lips but did not drink. You can label it classist if it makes you feel smart, he said loudly to Cotter. But when it comes down to it, those entrance exams are the fairest for everybody.

I label it classist because it is classist, Cotter replied with his back to Boner. Do you understand what you sound like? Honestly, Cotter choked, and he halted mid-step, faced Boner. Honestly, now. It tickled like a nettle scald to meet this intense stare, and so Boner scoffed, pretended to search for his phone in his many pockets. Do you think that? Cotter asked in a tiny voice, and Boner had to look up at him again.

After a second that did not feel like a second, Boner broke into an exaggerated howl. Then the three behind joined in. Will you calm down? Boner shouted to Cotter,

I'm only messing with you. Chuckling, Boner raised his hands as if it was a stick up. You get so mad, man, Boner said. Cotter didn't smile at this, didn't loosen his rigid stance and agree, instead he studied Boner before mumbling that he was going to the toilet.

As he stamped off towards the hedges that had been designated as the outdoor toilet, Cotter said quietly to Boner, You're still at this shit.

Boner just laughed.

If offered the chance, Boner would definitely for sure admit aloud he was glad to be back talking with Cotter. It was a shock earlier for Cotter to slink up as if nothing had happened, to start a conversation as if nothing thorny had transpired. Then again, the scrimmage over the house and its deposit had been stupid in the first place so perhaps it shouldn't have been a surprise? Maybe the surprise was that it had taken Cotter this long to get over it? The exact specifics of their fight were a little blurry to Boner, but ultimately how was it his fault his points rose by ten in the Leaving Cert rechecks and his course requirements fell by five? And how was it that since Boner's first choice was thus obtainable – if Boner wanted it, which clearly he did, it was his first choice – and he no longer needed to languish below in Galway that he should be guilted to pay for that manky house due to Cotter's fear of unknown housemates and, to be clear, the full deposit wasn't that much and Cotter didn't even stick at college for that long? Boner felt the buzzy ache of argument along his jawline, and he had to still himself. What's done is done and is squashed, Boner thought.

Sniffing, he sipped his can in respect of this wisdom.

Simon, Róisín, and Jamie were heading back inside and they gave a bright call to Boner, who waved to them without swinging around.

There was the shunt of the uncooperative sliding door.

The amplified cheers and singing from the house flew out and by. Boner heard excited yells, fits of laughter, then a lonely dog barking.

Eyeing Cotter's hunched shoulders now in amongst the hedges – he could never piss like everyone else, always awkward and prudish – Boner tested the slosh of his can and considered if he had the distance in his throw. Then he thought: Best not poke too much. He thought: It was good to see him. Anyhow, he likely didn't have the distance. On the grass before Boner was a slab of twenty-four cans – Simon had gone halves. Boner had smoke and a baggy in his lower left backpocket and Buckfast chilling to perfection in the fridge. He had nothing to do tomorrow but be hungover. And when Cotter ambled back, Boner tilted forward to gift him a can, explaining that Simon wouldn't mind at all. No worries.

Smoking a joint, Boner had asked questions about Cotter's folks, his cat Mandy – dead, truck – and whether he was still working in the hotel or, and now similar questions were being volleyed back his way, though with tagged-on queries about Dublin and the astrophysics and whether the clubs up there were that unreal. Boner answered these Dublin questions shortly but not, he felt, rudely, for he reckoned it wasn't nice for Cotter to dwell on college and all it entailed and all he had somehow banjaxed. And to move the conversation swiftly on, Boner was about to begin a spiel about the current malaise in guitar music – music being what had bonded them together in first year, the two moshers in a class of fifteen – when Cotter mentioned reapplying to college for September. Soc and Pol. In Dublin this time. Not for definite yet, but it was a big, big possibility, Cotter said, and he rubbed his mouth. Dublin probably suit me more, like, Cotter explained. To this idea, Boner emphatically encouraged: Oh, you should, man. You're well able. And Boner kept on talking then because it seemed to him extremely important to be talking, to be supportive, and arching forward in his chair, Boner invented a lad in his own course who had returned to college after a sad spell out, who retrieved his happy self and did spot on thereafter, and Boner was summarising the theory of chatting if you needed to chat when all of a sudden, and not at all fluidly, he was apologising to Cotter about the deposit, that silly stuff with the money. I should have paid it, Boner said, I know I should have. He was animated now, hands busy with gestures, and he was desperately seeking Cotter's gaze in the violet dusk. I'm sorry, I'm sorry about all that. And I'm sorry if you felt like I sort of left you behind, in the lurch, or anything, and, and, and you should reapply, Boner said, wincing, backtracking to what they were talking about in the first place. Why not, sure? Boner said. There was no immediate response to this outpouring, bar Cotter signalling for another can, which Simon's absence duly granted, and while this new can tssked suds, while Boner held his breath and weighed up conjuring a spare room in his sister's gaff in Dublin; his joint rolling unconsciously between his thumb and middlefinger, there came Cotter's reply. A simple, glottal, I might do, yeah. Before Boner could cheer him on again, Cotter checked over his shoulder and said: They have horses someplace around here. You heard that, yeah?

It was just after ten, no, it was quarter to eleven, and whenever people picked their way outside to the patio their shadows flickered spindly across Boner's spread feet, as if they were backed by a great big fire. He liked this. It reminded Boner of Christmas, though there was no fireplace in his house. So maybe not Christmas? Above, the sky was the blue of ink spilled in a white shirt pocket. Everything, in fact, was blue. The world whistled round Boner. Voices. Shrieks. He was a tad drunk now. He'd also agree he was whacked. Simon had been pissy over his depleted share of cans. That had happened, that was funny. And at one point, at some hazy point, Tara had crept over to them with a dog by her side. Crouching, holding Boner's armrest, then his arm, to steady herself, she thanked them both for coming, asked why weren't they inside?, said that this bold boy went toilet in the kitchen, thanked them both for coming, asked why weren't they inside? Then Tara wondered about Marian, her whereabouts in the house, who she could be chatting to, and said to Cotter with a mischievous inflection, I bet you're missing her already, aren't you? Cotter didn't answer and eventually, or was it straightaway, Tara floated off with the dog, and it was probably this mysterious lack of reply on Cotter's part, that inserted the subject of Marian in Boner's wavy mind, which compelled him to blurt a while later, What's the craic with you and the little lady?

How you mean? Cotter replied worryingly quickly.

Just. I don't know, Boner said, unsure himself what he truly meant. He knew they had started going out in January – Tara had told him that. Or at least they started shifting around then. And why had he called Marian a little lady? She was taller than Boner.

Like. How's everything going in the relationship? Boner corrected.

It's good, Cotter said sharply.

Ah, that is class, Boner said, and he was busy blowing out fluffy clouds when Cotter said, You know Marian's heading off? To London, like.

Boner said he had heard that, alright, though he was fairly sure he hadn't.

Well, she wants me to head over with her.

Yeah? Boner said. Music was playing from his phone. The Stones, 'Sway'. He had the makings of at least another two joints on his bunched knees. And are you going to? Boner asked when Cotter didn't elaborate. Go with her, I mean.

She begged me to, but, Cotter's answer tapered off into the sound of puffed cheeks. Boner squinted and made out his pal in the dark, watched him remove a hand from under his leg and dig it through his hair. Fuck that though, Cotter said and then quicker, I have no interest heading to

London. And I'll probably have college now in September. In Dublin. Yeah, no, I'm not going with her.

Let her off, Cotter continued after a moment, and Boner looked up from his dainty handiwork once more. There was mumbling or whispering now, and Boner had to bend forward to hear. Between me and you, the mumbling or whispering said, I was half-thinking of breaking it off with her, so, I'm kind of delighted, really. It works out for the best this way.

I'd feel bad otherwise.

For her, like.

She's nothing great, Cotter said, nothing at all special, and, honestly, her clothes aren't even that good, and Boner butted in here to steadfastly agree with his old friend so he could concentrate on flipping this immaculate joint.

To speed along the afternoon Cotter had a shower and afterwards, perched dripping on the corner of his bed, mulled over the evening laid in front of him, and in this absorbed state, ignored another phonecall. The two condoms – one in its ritzy blue wrapper, the other open and unrolled like shedded snakeskin – were on his desk. Also on the desk were booklets for various colleges and ITs, and two separate newspaper articles about the Guards seeking recruits in the new year. All deposited there by his dad. His phone vibrated on the windowsill, pinged to inform he had missed a call. Cotter wasn't sure why he was ignoring her or why he was sparking a confrontation between them and what benefit, if any, this may have for his plan. It had happened naturally enough: he woke and shunned her morning message because it was too early and then the next one at eleven and then the one after that and a call and then it was now.

His hair was a grainy brown, but when wet it turned to this crow colour. Cotter had been trying to grow it out for the last two months but to no success – his hair was too straight, the barber and then the hairdresser had explained – and so it reached the end of his neck, surfery and cool, while simultaneously mushrooming up and out from the centre of his head like a velvet riding helmet. He had also failed, in the last month or so, to sprout anything beyond weedy chin hair and some sparse whiskers on his face, which his manager had discreetly then publicly warned had to be sheared pronto. Cotter had plans for an ear piercing and a tattoo of twin swallows on his inner bicep. He was going to go interrailing. His laptop was currently shuffling through his 'sad rain MOOD' playlist. The tabs on Chrome were riddled with the prettiest photos of Marian pasted from Facebook. He stood and looked at the condoms, selected the open one – pinching it sideways with his finger and thumb as if it were a glass slide – and headed back out to the bathroom.

First, he shaved his chin and upper lip, which took less than a minute. Then he gripped the sink and breathed in and out till he was lightheaded. It was decided, he had decided, and yet there was this something today obstructing his previous clarity. It was like hair clogged in a shower's drain: it didn't halt him, but it did hinder his mind from flowing precisely. He didn't think it was guilt, this blockage. It wasn't guilt, but maybe it was too much kindness? The expanse of his kindness and how it would not rightaway be valued as kindness? He spat into the sink. It was the correct course of action; he was sure of that.

He thumped his fist against his chest. Exhaled.

He attached the condom to the spout of the tap and twisted it on. A few drips at first and he twisted it slightly more and the condom filled – this birdbeck shape at the crucial cocked point, the bubbles pipping inside – until water began to spurt out in shoots from the end. The tap was turned off. He inspected the condom, leaning in and out. He noted scrupulously where the five holes were situated. The quantity of liquid that squirted. And once sure he had learned off where each incision was on the latex, once satisfied with the volume freed, he unplugged the condom.

Cocooned within toilet paper, he flushed it.

He dressed – blacks jeans, a tatty jersey with Tevez on the back – and, sitting at his desk, he took up the thumbtack, tore the blue wrapper, and copied his earlier work. The johnny offered small squeaks of resistance. Fleeting sunlight arrived through the window, heated one side of his face, and went out. He couldn't have gone with her to London. Realistically, how could he? How could he unravel himself from everything here? The job, his folks, his other commitments no matter how seemingly small or insignificant: the five-a-side league; his aunt's jeep that could be his in the nearable future; Nana, now that she was older, and Nana's dogs now that she was older. It was easy for Marian, or at least so she assumed, but not for him. It was impossible for him. How could he leave? Did she ever think about that? His mam shouted up, then his dad, and he replied to both when it was completed and the condom – smushed once more inside its wrapper – was in his jacket's inner compartment. Snatching his phone, he went downstairs and ate and typed a semi-apology that morphed into a lengthy fib about an elderly neighbour who had tripped in the night, about assisting his dad with said neighbour, who, by the way, was a woman and widowed. It was an unattackable alibi, Cotter felt.

In the next message, he said he'd ring her.

Then in his room, he sent: Sure I'll just see you later at Taras?

He lay on his bed.

Around seven, he awoke to a text that she was sorry to hear about his neighbour. How was she now? But he could have said something no? Rung her back? A time later, she sent another message that read: You'll head up to the party soon? Its v boring atm!! Just me and Tara's mates. He bit his thumbnail. His rainjacket was folded over the chair by the desk. Her favourite shirt hung on the door handle, washed and ironed. To think she hadn't hinted he should go with her. It wasn't remotely on her mind. How nasty. How unfair.

Cotter replied and it read: yeah I will yeah.

# The First Real Time

The first is efficient, mature: 'Hey xx i have a free house Friday ... Wanna come over ?'

It only took you four drafts.

The second text is written five minutes later, after chewing on the edge of your baby finger, after stomping downstairs and peering into the fridge and cupboards, after retrieving the phone from where you had flung it on the carpeted floor. It is blasé, indifferent, shitting-itself: 'If u want to.'

You press send without looking and immediately a structure bends in the gooey pit of your stomach and you turn off the phone and turn it on again and pace your box room and hate yourself deeply and wait and wait and wait.

Of course, you've kissed others. At discos, or in the front row of the cinema, or while standing on a broken pallet behind Lavelle's; your tipsy right hand ambitiously hiking up inside a zipped-tight fleece. At a houseparty over the Christmas you even managed sex with a red-cheeked college home-comer named Hannah Heron. An exhausting ten minutes spent flexing your calves to stone and thinking how the plastic snowflakes dangling across the fireplace looked more like rotting teeth than glistening snow. When Hannah asked if you could get off her now please, you pretended to come at that exact second of instruction because, you guessed, it would be rude otherwise. It would be bad form otherwise. But Emily, you tell your sticky private self, is different. She is the first girl you've kissed more than once, kissed when it wasn't dark or sweaty-walled or thrumming with noise. Special, you've decided she is special.

It started when an informer let it be known that she – somehow – fancied you. She was a year younger, fresh, and you were aware of her from narrow corridors and assemblies. In reply to the news, you had only shrugged and muttered sounds like 'whatever', 'yeah?' and 'who?' You then spent the rest of the week strategically clomping past her locker, roundish belly sucked in and chest tensed, in the pretence of checking the football corkboard. You couldn't talk face-to-face, obviously, so you messaged her online, chatting with shattered punctuation and three-quarter spelling. Eventually, you arranged to meet down the laneway by Keel beach. A Sunday in February, smoky and dry with copper hinted beneath cloud, and you were early, apparently calm, apparently collected, and her arms were crossed as she turned the corner and you said, 'Emily,' and it seemed then you were playing a game to discover who could avoid eye contact the longest. You talked vaguely about school, the Leaving, weekend jobs, school again, all the while marching towards the cover of the playground, where, pressed against the climbing wall, you finally licked the face off one another. Afterward, walking home, your chest echoed dully like evidence, your skin glowed.

Since then you've been meeting her semi-regularly after school in the basketball court. She's not your girlfriend, technically, but for the last five weeks you've been *with* her. That distinction has been sealed. You know nothing much about her other than that her skin is the colour of streetlamp against wet pavement, and that when she cracks a proper smile a suicide-edged snaggletooth peeks out. You presume this is all you need to know about her, this is how it works. When together, when between kisses, you act as if you're interviewing for a job you don't truly want, securely jailing all mentions of PlayStation games, the music you actually listen to, your tabletop Elven army, your membership of an online forum for divorcees.

Sometimes, alone, you fantasise about putting yourself in physical peril for her safety, of being wounded in front of her (preferably a superficial gash, preferably because of her idiotic mistake), but mostly, alone, you hate the thought of others pairing you together, you hate the thought of admitting you view her as something precious. You're ashamed in case she doesn't measure up in their estimates. You're scared that she isn't good enough, though you're not exactly sure who she isn't good enough for. You insist these are normal fears. This is normal behaviour.

It isn't till the next morning – a Thursday – that you receive Emily's answer to your invitation: 'maybe'.

Followed quickly by another rumble: 'But ask in person next time!!'

You breathe again. Life can be so very beautiful. Before the first class of the day, Maths with Conroy, you compose a steely reply, 'will do', and then daring yourself add a ';)'. It feels like a significant weight has been lifted. It feels like a significant weight has been piled onto your shoulders.

At lunchtime, you roost with the lads as normal. By the far far wall, defaced by chalked names, its slim crevices treasured with crisp packets. Cigarettes are shared, tabs of Coke cans tssked, gelled skulls bob, and abuse bleeds over silence. The crew's currency is what you have done versus what you haven't. Alcohol, smoking, petty drugs, and the laddersteps of sex grant privilege. Allow you to escape slagging, nicknames, being pathetic at sports. But that means you have to cash in when presented with an opportunity. That means you must tell them about her and the free house.

Throughout lunch, you loiter in the borders of conversation. Laughing only at the safe jokes, agreeing heartily about who is a wanker and who isn't, and, when possible, siding with Mitch – the leader. As wrappers are tossed down by dandelions, as chat swings to the burden of afternoon French, you feel your stomach tighten, this clench between ribs, and you decide it would be best to stall, to tell them when you hear the bell. Less time, you figure, for interrogation. For mockery. And when the bell eventually sounds – wide and strangely chirpy and too soon to your ears – and the lads crank their shoulders and begin the theatrical process of strolling towards class, you blurt it out. Blunt as a mirror in the morning.

'Yeah, so,' you say, scuffing the ground with a heel-drag. 'Yeah, so, she's coming over tomorrow.'

Faint sunlight on your neck.

In the surrounding trees crows squabble and beyond the glazed windows, the dreary screech of chairs hauled out from under desk.

Within the group a moment of headtilts, sniffy nostrils, tetchiness, as the lads turn inward and reflect quietly on this information and on their own wet failures, their own staleness in comparison, a moment thawed only when Mitch pucks you on the arm and winks: 'Fuckin Casanova here! You kept that one under your blanket.'

The rest pile in then. Voices bright and filled with taunts, best wishes and professional advice. 'Nice one', 'fair play' and 'johnny'.

Modestly, you fend off their enquiries. You spit out a dangling web and it lands on your own runner, but you're unfazed. 'Might as well, like,' you say.

The lads whoop. They call Emily names. Cruel names, but you don't correct them. No. Instead you snigger along as triumph knocks heavy in your chest.

When you arrive home that evening, your mother is sat in front of the box. By her feet are three or four stacked mugs. The only light in the room is the intermittent blink of the television.

In the same breath you cry hello, you wonder about dinner.

She says there is risotto on the counter.

You thank her and retrieve a pizza from the freezer.

Over the last three months, you've noticed how the cuffs of your mother's woollen jumpers have become flecked with hardened chips of paint, how her hair, unkempt and long, has started to grey. MammyMayo, a regular on the forum, often says that your general appearance is important, both for immediate healing and, in time, for a new vibrant future.

After setting the oven, you check the fridge and wearily count the three cartons of milk. A glass windchime sings, the curtains aren't pulled closed.

From the doorway, you ask what's on the telly, though you know the answer.

She swivels, smiles at you with squared teeth: 'Judge Judy.' She has every series recorded and watches the episodes nightly in three-hour blocks. 'It's a good one, too,' she says.

'You went to the shop?'

The back of her head nods.

Your fingernail picks absently at the wooden door-frame, the cream paint wrinkled and crunchy, as you fumble with the next question: 'Did you get much work done today?'

'Not today,' she responds cheerfully. 'No, not today.'

The TV gets louder.

'The people are real,' a voice booms. 'The cases are real.'

Rarely now does she venture out to the glasshouse, her studio, disordered with clay and plastic buckets and woven sacks. Rarely now does she seek your approval of her creations, casts of women with bull horns. You understand from the forum that neglecting your work is not a great sign. You're reminded of what Debbie67 says about bad days. Bad days can morph into bad months if you're not careful. You could be experiencing a spell of the sorrys without even realising it. The sorrys, Debbie67 writes, are not an example of positive defiance. The sorrys are, in fact, the opposite of positive defiance.

Hunched on the stairs, you eat the pizza and watch your mother watching the TV. The house is free tomorrow because she is heading to one of her hippie conventions. Where flocks of twig-heads gather in a field to pound on African drums, hum communally, purchase crystals and beeswax soap, and stretch out their glutes. She invited you along last summer. To Clare. Where you munched a veggie dog, had your face painted, flirted badly with a mother of four, smoked a joint that tasted of paraffin, and then spewed up as everyone clapped around a fire. In the car, you pleaded food poisoning. She narrowed her eyes and asked, 'Do you think I'm stupid?'

When she mentioned she mightn't attend this one – it was such short notice, she said, I have nothing planned – you reminded her how much she loved these weekends, how all her friends would be there, that you'd be fine on your own, that she must go. Your intentions only partially selfish. OK, she said with a convinced tut, OK, OK, OK. She was happy, you were both happy, until a question, an impulse, slipped from your lips: 'Sure, Dad could be around anyway?' Instantly you regretted the question. Her face grew slack like an unmade bed.

'We'll see,' she replied after what felt an age. 'Maybe. We'll see.'

While rinsing the plate, you decide tonight you want to watch TV with her. Keep her company. You want to keep her company. Or maybe you want to quell the itch of doing something without her permission. But what difference does motive make here? She smiles when you perch beside her. 'Howdy, partner,' she whispers inexplicably.

During the last case, involving a buck in a fat-collared lime shirt and his former partner, your mother starts to chuckle dryly, grinning. They are disputing over rent and a VCR and she says: 'Please, don't ever end up like them anyway.' You let out a smirk, glance at her and then your phone. She is running her bauble necklace between thumb and forefinger. 'Listen to him,' she says, skitting. 'Judy has him figured. Wait now. She'll eat him in a minute.'

On cue the lime-shirted man struggles over the particular date of a particular payment and Judy explodes.

You produce a single, conforming, 'Ha.'

'What did I tell you?' your mother says.

You offer another laugh.

'You must think I'm desperate,' she says then, without looking at you. Her voice is uneven and you hold your breath, command yourself to stare directly ahead, only at the screen. Your right hand withers into a fist. You want the TV to blow, the walls to crumble, the roof to buckle.

The credits finally flash, the rosegold titles staining the carpet to rust, and you hurry to excuse yourself, declaring that you'd better head to bed. It's late. It's a school night. You have study to do.

Your mother nods, pains a smile, and you can see her tongue, bunched as it is between upper and lower teeth. A quirk of hers. 'There, there,' she says.

After hesitating for a moment, you peck her cheek, Night, and then go upstairs. You wonder: Why can't she be dignified?

In your room, you try to distract yourself by hitting on the PlayStation. Find a reprieve in guns and carjacking. But thoughts tickle the inside of your head. You recall your mother, drunk at her fortieth, saying she should have flown back to Frankfurt, should have gone back to real art. You recall your father pinching the bulge of his nose as you drove home from Mass at Christmas and the peculiar, tight silence in the car. Were these signs you should have been able to read? Should it have occurred to you earlier? You shut off the PlayStation and walk to the bathroom. There, you turn on the hot tap and drown your face for a minute at a time. Steam ghosts the mirror, your cheeks appear rashy as if nettlestung, but the water seems to you mild. In bed, you toss about the sheets until you feel numb, drained. You text

Emily then, the green of the lit screen softening, soothing. You send messages like 'Xxxx', 'WUA', ':)' and 'hahah'.


Over breakfast, your mother goes through the protocol for the free house, marking each on a separate finger:

Lasagne will be made.

Just-in-case money will be under the fruit bowl.

A spare key will be left by the back door.

A phonecall will arrive at half-nine and it will be answered at half-nine.

She concludes with warnings against parties, shadowy gallivanting and the potential dangers of the hob, using words like 'don't' and 'dare'.

You nod when appropriate, spooning more cornflakes into your gob. Your mind whirring. Already savage. Already horny.


In school, your Friday is focused on avoiding her. At short break, you sag from the group when you reckon she might be over at the shop. During the stroll between French and History you perform an anti-clockwise loop to dodge her leaving English. You can't face facing her. But during the afternoon you clock her figure fifteen feet ahead, braced against a discoloured radiator. You're beside Dicey, plodding towards Mr Kelly's class, a bag slung on one shoulder. You realise immediately there is no alternative backroute, no chance to reverse and hide by your locker until she saunters past.

You have to continue forward.

The hallway is echoes and yells and the rubber-squeak of runners. The two-minute turmoil between classes, the smell of mint gum, lozenges and afternoon underarm.

A light blazes in from the window, graphing the floor into squares.

In your head you rapidly prepare greetings, visualise yourself opening your mouth and saying, 'Hello, what you at?' Maybe giving her a thumbs-up. A thumbs-up would be cool.

You then glance at her.

Her navy cotton socks stretch below the face of her knees. She is holding a purple folder to her chest. Her hair is loose, clearly straightened. Her Converse are untied, the left foot arched just so.

Jesus Christ.

You bite hard the inside of your cheek and, passing her, choke out a scrawny, 'Howya.' No eye contact, of course, but you do flinch a sharp, gentlemanly nod.

'Hey,' she says, smiling without showing teeth. A nearly imperceptible smile.

You pretend not to hear her friend's teasing squeal as you wheel into the classroom, you pretend not to feel your face boil to scarlet as girls in your year gawk at you and then her, and as you lurch down to your desk, you tell an oooing Dicey to shut his fuckin hole quickish.

After school, you hitch a lift with a neighbour, jangle out key from flower pot, sling bag under the stairs, and remove lasagne from the oven.

Despite feeling no hunger, you gouge down a banana. Glucose.

Upstairs, you model in front of the floor-length sliding mirror, slanting your hips to gain more impressive angles while diligently picking apart your faults: the crusted pimples on your chin, the blackheads pocked on your snout, the unfixable shitness of your hair. You put on a navy T-shirt and then take it off and put on a plain white T-shirt and then take it off and put back on the navy T-shirt. The thought strikes that perhaps this is some elaborate prank, organised by the lads. That it's some sick game. You laugh this off, it's a ridiculous notion, comical, and then, via the spareroom, you scan the garden for cameras or bodies cowering in the shrubs. This is normal behaviour.

Your phone vibrates, mooing against the woodgrain desk. For a moment, you freak – she is early, why is she early – but unlocking the phone you discover it's only from your dad. A picture message: a sleeping bag curled beneath a table, alongside a space heater, a chunky cord lead, and the mini-radio you helped pick out last weekend. It reads: 'Cosy with my new radio !' For six weeks solid, your dad has been camping in his dentistry in Castlebar. At first, he said it was to avoid the morning traffic. But then weeknights spilled into the weekend and everyone acted as if nothing had changed.

You reply with a smiley face. There is nothing else to say.

Preparation: You brush your teeth, guzzle your mother's mouthwash, slap your face with your mother's moisturiser, smother yourself in Lynx Africa, and then conclude that now would be the optimum time to trim your pubes. With the vibrating blade, you scud along the curly dark lawn and then skim the fluffy, bally base. When you're done, your groin is gritty with black stitches, full of wayward corkscrews, and your dick isn't ten times larger. You clean some of the noticeable blood, curse your handiwork, and then curse the squiggle patches of hair on your chest, the question marks around each nipple. When you were nine you wanted to shave your newly fuzzy legs. Your father burst into hysterics when you requested a razor. 'You're becoming a man,' he exclaimed with arms akimbo, 'you've nothing to be ashamed of.'

There is something very wrong with you.

You strip posters from your bedroom walls: a staff-wielding Gandalf, the boys walking across Abbey Road. With a shovel-edged hand, you breeze away the creases on your quilt before worrying because said quilt is decorated with teenaged turtles. You hope she won't notice or, better yet, that she won't notice you. You long for her to not even look at you. That perhaps she might shut her eyes throughout and you would guide her and it will happen without effort on your part. That it will run smooth as water along glass and when it's over, neither of you will be able to pinpoint how it exactly happened. But, also, neither of you will be able to pinpoint where it spun wrong. It will just have occurred. You feel like a serial killer thinking this.

You instruct yourself to relax. You change into a maroon jumper. You spray more Lynx.

Your phone goes off again and you lunge for it and then almost fling it against the wall when you glimpse 'dad'. A text this time: 'new radio courtesy of my son !'.

Who else is he sending these messages to?

You don't reply and you delete both of his messages with only a smudge of shame, arguing that you need to conserve memory, battery.

In the half hour before she's due to arrive you position the untuned guitar against the radiator in your room, you construct a stable route of conversation in your head, you count and recount the condoms in the drawer. At six o'clock, you hear a car, squint at the sulphur flash of headlights through your window. You wait for the text, the rasp on the desk, and pound the stairs when it comes: 'here x'.

Outside, the sky is the colour of damp denim. The dark of oncoming night has already begun to taper the corners of the world, but Emily shines clean as she steps from her sister's Toyota. She talks through the passenger window, her posture hunchbacked, her sister glaring in your direction. By the interior light Emily's face is pink, pinkish, and she turns briefly around – are you supposed to wave? – before resuming her discussion with the sister.

You listen to the arid mechanics of your own body, the rattle of your lungs, the stammered breath, the swooning in your chest.

Then Emily glides towards you as if it's simple. The car grudgingly reverses.

She has done it before. With an older boy, she told you

after you pushed. Forehead pressed against her bunched knees, she confided in you about being drunk and dumb and not being able to say no. You listened with deliberately timed sighs. When she wept, you patted her shoulder, reassured her it was OK, all OK, despite rank jealousy caking your tongue. 'I wish I hadn't,' she said then, 'I really wish I hadn't. He was a fucking asshole.' Later, alone, you will think again about this, about her first time, and fury will flame and you will call her a slut. It was her story and yet you will manage to gouge yourself with it. You will deduce that it ultimately really scalds you more.

At the door, Emily says hey and then eases by you. You forget how to say hello. She peels off her jacket – the fabric whistling free from her arms. She is in her uniform still and you feel wholly unprepared as you lock the door.

She treads behind as you give a tour of the house. She touches things and asks fleeting, incomplete questions like 'When did you …?' 'Is that …?' 'Who is …?' You answer swiftly, jumping close to the item in question, consciously brushing nearer to her.

In the sitting room, she drifts along the corner table, her finger skimming photo frames. Swirling alive dust motes. You watch her pick up a photograph, tilting it towards herself.

She laughs, softly, and shoves it at you.

It's a family portrait: the three of you arranged like unpacked Russian Dolls against a fading backdrop, black to wine to muddy gold. It was taken ten years ago, when you were seven and had the physique of the Michelin Man.

She says, 'Your mom's really pretty.'

You reply after a moment, 'She's a fuckin hippie'. The aggression a surprise to you.

You replace the photograph.

Her nose wrinkles. 'Don't say that,' she says.

'Well,' you shrug, 'it's true.'

She doesn't reply, goes instead to the couch. You join her, contorting your legs so your thighs don't touch. Not yet.

You begin to flick through the channels, stopping at the news – you don't want anything too stimulating. 'This alright?'

She crosses her legs but says nothing. A heat radiates from her. You try to smile normally, sit normally, but your body is fidgeting, fighting, you find a new rickety variation in how you exhale. The mood is unexpectedly formal, dangerous. You recall jokes – bad, sappy jokes – and tell them, and in return she only gifts you this pinched-mouth, no-teeth smile. It could be a frown, you suppose, hard to split the difference between them, but you assure yourself, nipping your jumper from your stomach, it was a smile. Not to worry about it, you reason, it had to be a smile. Not to analyse it, it must be a smile.

Nothing is said. A minute, then another, crawls by.

On the TV, Obama is speaking. You point with the remote. 'He's great, isn't he?'

She nods, seems to consider something more, something deeper, but only answers, 'Yep.'

Why is it difficult now?

'Yeah,' you say. 'Obama's sound. He's a sound man.'

She leans forward and rummages in her handbag and then sits back.

You can count how many buttons are undone on her shirt and you do count and suddenly you feel yourself get a horn, a judging heat, and you fold your arms and jut out your chest. *So, Now You're The Big Man*, the paperback left on your pillow for your twelfth birthday, suggests visualising doing the gardening to rid yourself of any pesky, undesired erections. You do this now; you envision clipping the hedges but then she hums and readjusts a leg and you are trampled. You surely can't fuck this up? And yet here you are, fucking it up, dreaming about hedges. You beg yourself now to do something, to act, and you start imagining potentially enticing actions – a hand on her thigh; an arm dipped sensually over her shoulder; a proposal to show her your guitar, maybe strum a G chord or two – and you're thinking about all this when she turns, smiles with teeth, and kisses you.

Her tongue is sugary. You store your hands by your side and kiss and kiss and kiss until she pulls away. Everything is amplified; the cushions rustle like woodlice, the TV nags. You feel empty, delightfully empty. With a lifted chin, you motion upstairs. She says something, nods, gathers her bag and then decides to leave it on the floor. In your chest, there is a gasping excitement. You stand and your hands are shaking so you slot them into your pockets and claw at the inside fabric. You study the ceiling as you lead the way, noting precisely where the paint is wonky, not quite in line.

She sits on the bed, a knee hugged under her chin. You draw the curtains. From the corner of your eye, you watch as she inspects a spot on her knee, working her thumbnail against it before rubbing the spot with the heel of her hand. You like this. You punch off the lights, deeming darkness, partial invisibility, a valuable ally. On the bed, you cockroach near her, maintaining a forearm's width between you both.

The air feels trapped and impure and somewhere in it there is the fragrance of cinnamon.

Mellow light burns beneath the doorframe.

Her leg drops to the floor, she grabs her upper arms as if cold.

You take long breaths through your nose to shush the thump and throw of your body and then, while thinking about it an incredible amount, you take her hand and face her. It throws you for some reason that she stares back – what did you expect? – and then you lean in and clatter into her front teeth.

You apologise and she apologises and you both reshape, hunching toward one another – you feel her fingers guide your jaw and then feel how her lower lip is chapped. Cautiously, you let your hand cup the hurl-head of her hip. Loving it. You fall sideways together and bump together and the duvet is cumbersome. The air becomes thick like you could pack it in a bag. With assistance, the clip of her bra is unhooked. Her hand, her left hand, lies on your stomach and you will it to go down.

Your fingers spider open the zipper of her skirt and you graze, with the flat of your thumb, the bristles around her slit.

'Go easy,' she whispers.

You open your eyes to make sure this is real and say sorry.

'It's OK,' she says, and then, close to your ear, asks if you have condoms.

You nod. 'Yes.'

'Well,' she says, 'just go easy remember.'

You say sorry again.

You reach for the drawer, grasp a square of cartoon-blue foil. On bended knees, you chuck your jumper and then awkwardly shimmy off your pants. Socks are forgotten. You shrug the condom on and race on top of her once more, kissing her now, moving with her, and, on a sexy spur, you lick her collarbone.

'What are you doing?' She is laughing.

You sputter another apology. Eroticism is live and learn. She grabs you then, bends you, and it starts to be good.

As you work together, your limbs aren't silky, they aren't naturally posed to one other's range, but rather they work like levers. A jerk, a pull. A certain stubbornness of muscle, friction. You feel the tingle of her hot skin, the sweat. Her breath catches. The business is hurried and not slowed or savoured or graceful, it is done as if a timer is beeping somewhere. As if you're both on the verge of being found out.

You roll apart afterwards. No comments are exchanged, no critiques or acknowledgments. You lie as far from one another as possible on a queen-sized bed. Is there ever any pleasure in this? Your body is unfamiliar, gangly as if you have grown.

You stare at the ceiling, the curtains.

There is nothing to say.

She's probably pregnant now, you think.

On the divorcee forum, lynn62 recommends new activities, hobbies, trips. You've got to keep yourself busy. She uses phrases like Positive Thinking, the half-full glass, show the world what they're missing. You encourage your mother to go to hippie conventions, apply for residencies, you ask questions about art and her fave, Bernini. You tell your dad that you want to learn to drive, that suddenly you love teeth and dental hygiene. You WhatsApp him possible movie outings years in advance – 'New Batman 2020'. He dings an immediate reply, 'I'm on it,' as if it were a challenge, as if you wanted him to direct.

Emily begins mapping the birthmarks and moles on your shoulders, on the hairless topmost section of your arm. It feels like she is touching tendon, bone and all. The tantalising sensation of an oncoming storm. Slowly, she engraves her name and then yours and you wish that one moment could last.

It's then the car crunches up the driveway.

She puts a hand to her lips and her voice says things like, 'Who's that?', 'Shit', 'Where's my?'

A key is jammed into the lock, the scuttle of letters being fished from the wicker basket. You recognise the weight of the footsteps.

She sweeps up her clothes and for the first time you see her frightened, pissed off – her voice spiky, her gestures accelerated.

'Wait here,' you tell her, lugging on pants. You're the hero.

You pad down the stairs, a hand caressing the banister as a show of nonchalance, and spy him drinking milk straight from the carton in the kitchen. He isn't wearing his glasses. He hasn't shaved the goatee.

'Oh, you're here?' your father says. 'I thought you'd be at a pal's house.'

'Mam's gone to one of her hippie things.' You pause on the threshold to the kitchen. He already knows she is away, you understand that. He scoffs at the word 'hippie', says it to himself while placing his key on the counter beside the worn, peeling gym bag. There is a delay in your father's movement, a dilemma: should he keep drinking from the carton or pour himself a glass?

'You're home?' you say.

He sort of smiles, folds bridging his mouth. 'Not quite.' He takes a long gulp from the carton, puts it back in the fridge, and snags hold of the gym bag. You should scramble for the handle too, make a scene. Pull a tantrum. Call him a dickhead, a traitor. Scream nonsensically: You're not my real dad! But you don't react. 'Need to re-supply,' he says. 'But I will be home soon. Once work quietens.'

He lifts the bag. 'Is it just you here?'

Together you pack towels, shampoo, five shirts, three jumpers, Speedos, facial creams, two polos. You carry his shirts on hangers to the car, fold his pants onto the backseat, and neatly stash his shoes in the boot. It takes twenty minutes. You grin at your father's predictable gags and he listens as you describe the High Elf archer set you've ordered. He acts impressed, regurgitates information he swiped from a manual. 'Increased range,' he says with a raised finger. He has only shown interest in the game because you play it and this, even now, makes you glad.

When everything is packed, he mentions Sunday. 'That new superhero is out, isn't it?' He clicks his fingers. 'The Iron Man.' He climbs into the car and says in a mock, deepening voice, 'Be good for your mother, son.'

You tell him: 'Stall a sec.'

You rush inside and, without thinking, shoddily wrap in tinfoil the lasagne. It is somehow essential, this offering, though you can't decipher why.

'Mam made you this,' you say, you lie. You hand him the still-warm dish through the car window.

'Oh. Well, that was very nice of her.' He places the lasagne in the passenger seat and then has to buckle it in when a sensor starts beeping. You can't decide whose turn it is to speak, and before you can come to a conclusion, he gestures a thumbs-up and closes the window. Neither of you thought to switch on the outside lights, the pale-blue bulbs which flank the driveway, so in darkness you wave goodbye. He beeps once. For some time you stand there.

Back in the room, she is dressed and insane with questions. Her phone is beside her, alive with texts from friends who always suspected you were a weirdo. 'Who was

it?' she says, 'Did you tell them I was here?' You notice
she has made the bed and this astonishes you. 'You said
no one would be home. For fuck sake, John.' Her face is
screwed up and you don't say anything until she shifts close
to you, closer to you, and then you clutch her hand and
utter words like: 'please', 'don't', 'go'.

She doesn't and it is only months later, as summer begins,
that you fuck it up, that you let her go. You're official by
then, girlfriend and boyfriend with an x assigned by her
name in your phone. But at some shitshow of a disco you
will kiss someone else, tussle with a foreign tongue. And
during Emily's break up speech, you will pretend that
you're sad, depressed even, producing moody, music-video
faces. On the same day you break up, you will go meet the
girl you cheated on Emily with. And before the end of the
summer, you will beg Emily to take you back – the lust for
the cheating girl long dust at that stage. You will say you
were a fool, a mong, you will plead, you will even cry and it
will be no act this time. And Emily will say no, she will take
supreme pleasure in saying no, and you will inform your
friends that you don't care, she was a dirt anyway, and then
egg her house in a drunken stupor of weepy hate and weepy
love. No charges will be brought but her older brother will
thump open your nose on New Year's Eve. When you ship
off to college you will forget her for the most part, her
name only cropping up on Facebook when you're drunk
and nostalgic. You will message her once, during second
year as essay deadlines pile up, asking how's she getting

on. She will click on the message and you will tell yourself she only forgot to reply. And years later, when your mam and dad have met other people, when you celebrate two Christmases, when you have scampered off to the States to get lost, you will tell friends the story of your first time during a party. A wine bottle pointed in your direction, you will tell your new friends and the new girl who has the x by her name about that free house, about slanting your guitar in a bid to impress her with artistic flair in the same way you will now stack books by Benjamin and Borges and Woolf in an ordered messy pile in your apartment, about the colliding of front teeth, about your jangling nerves, about it being your first time. The friends will howl, your new girlfriend will feign envy with a pout, and you will spin the bottle and laugh as it points to somebody else. And at that moment, you will believe it was your first time, truly believe that she was your first real time.

# Twelve Pubs

Eugene Masterson had come to badly hate himself, which, he guessed, inevitably happened when you hated the digits in your bank account and your new north-facing single room below an hilariously randy couple and the extensive event called life-in-general, but wasn't it the day before Christmas eve and they were home, his two fadó fadó friends, the brothers Adrian and Mattie McNulty, and so tonight, with their benign company, and the small assistance from six litres of alcohol, self-loathing could be paused and familiar merriment resumed and maybe even something akin to solace felt up. They had, so far, completed three of the twelve pubs – Rooney's, Nolan's, The Crack in the Scaffolding – and were now hopping towards Lynott's Bar and Eatery: a sinking thatched roof, a rubble façade, and a tourist-friendly emerald door with a brass handle which stung Eugene's palm as he lugged it back: Mattie staggered by him on the one foot, breathing from his mouth, while Adrian walked and pouted and retrieved an arm from his Tommy bomber jacket. Inside was an older crowd, three greying couples, canes, a wheelchair, and the owner, Ted Lynott, peeling apart a newspaper on the large maple counter. A holly branch was taped to the toilet door, browning tinsel tangled about a Guide Dog collection tin. 'You're flat out, anyways,' Adrian called, and Ted looked up, gob ajar. Eugene laughed hard at this, adding, 'Not much work, being done in here, I see?' Mattie muttered, 'Good one, Eug.' Over the mottled cash register, the clock read ten past six and thankfully, the drink was starting to hit. Anticipation, Eugene knew, would soon be overtaken. Relief, humour, undepressing thoughts, fun, numbness, oblivion, excitement: they were at the precipice and it was all before them. They shook hands with Ted and sat themselves on the ripped and sticky stools and then, as one, the men ordered.

As the pints were being pulled, Mattie explained the rule for this establishment: you may drink with the left hand only. Eugene giggled. Adrian sighed and said, 'What is with these rules?' Eugene giggled at this, too. A radio was playing swooning, orchestral versions of Christmas carols and now a posh voice was breaking over. The pong of talcum powder and wax and straight vodka. Eugene was twenty-nine and he was wearing a woollen jumper emblazoned with a beer-guzzling Santa in sunglasses and Hawaiian shorts – the Santa lit up, briefly, when a button was thumbed in the sleeve – and beneath this jumper, a freshly ironed shirt. Mattie was a year younger, dimpled chin, striking blue eyes, and he wore a bicep-suffocating polo shirt and a Santa hat. Adrian was the eldest by two years, stocky, receding hairline like a hastily refigured national border, and a stubbly beard that did not agree with his skin. All three wore dark navy jeans with generous cuffs that tapered over the laces of their bright leather dress shoes.

Adrian turned to the couples by the wall. 'Well, this is depressing,' he said, loudly.

Mattie smirked, 'Get over it, man.'

One by one, the glasses were placed shakily in front of the men: the heads solid and white like overnight snow gathered in the cleavage of a stone wall, and Eugene wanted to say this aloud, or to say that he finds himself staring at the bare wall in his bedroom willing for a release from whatever force is crushing his brain and isn't that classic Eugene Masterson, but instead he said: Teddy, how are you still alive?

It was a decent joke. Six out of ten.

The men talked about things they had talked about – how the brothers were getting on in the States, if their football was still going, the scandalous amount of money they were raking in, how Eugene was better off without Sonia – and they drank steadily. People queued to the left of the men when they ordered – a small few said hello, wished them a Merry Christmas. Sinatra was singing. 'So, all going well over there?' Eugene asked for possibly the fourth time that evening. Mattie checked his phone and Adrian answered for them both, 'No complaints.' Adrian's hands were steepled together on the counter and he was looking at Eugene through the greasy mirror behind the bar. 'Happy out,' Adrian said, and Eugene nodded, gulped stout.

There had been a bad incident one night – a bottle had met someone's face – and for that, depending on who you believed, the McNulty brothers had been booted from the Island and the country. But, in reality, they were escaping anyway: jobs had been sorted in an uncle's landscaping business, they had inherited the correct passport, and so the incident and fallout were mere acceleration, if anything. It was seven years ago now, which didn't make sense to Eugene. Where did the time go? And why did it not feel like time went anywhere? And was this a holy or scientific or economic conundrum?

Still engrossed in his phone, Mattie raised his glass and Eugene snapped, 'Right hand'.

Howls at this. Eugene found himself fist pumping momentarily.

Theatrical despair from Mattie – he was a good sport – and his punishment was buying a round of shots.

A shudder after Eugene downed his little glass of amber, and he delighted in sharing this revulsion with Adrian. Mattie then bought one for Ted Lynott, who protested, indicated his feeble heart and his many recent heart attacks. 'Drink to fuck, Ted,' Eugene goaded, and the brothers laughed, and this was exactly what Eugene needed. It was what the doctor had ordered, though he had not gone to the doctor in the end, despite his mother's begging.

They were neighbours growing up, a lumpy bronze field separating their houses out in Curran, and they were inseparable school friends – Eugene was a bit of a liar but the brothers were kings in secondary school and acted as insulation from backlash and mockery – and then they were a means for each other to escape – to drink, to cruise about in Adrian's Mitsubishi, to have something to do – and now they were what essentially tied one another to the Island, beyond their parents and headstones. Sonia had asked him once who he preferred out of the two bold brothers, and the thought had never crossed Eugene's mind before. He tried to explain to her that he preferred neither. They were just his best friends – both, together, two-for-one.

'What you make of Mourinho, anyhow?' Adrian asked Eugene.

A puffy fella with a limp was limping his way to the toilet, and Mattie stopped him by leaning back in the stool and using his head as a roadblock. 'Coleman,' Mattie said. The gentleman swivelled and after a moment offered a pink hand. 'Ah, Matthew, sorry. I didn't see you there.'

Eugene went on, 'Maybe José is past it. The game has evolved. Fair enough. But those lads aren't good enough for United. And is that his fault, too?'

'Watch,' Adrian said in the mirror.

Mattie took the man's extended hand in his own two, shook it vigorously, and Eugene felt his toes slowly curl. He waited.

'And how's the shop looking these days?' Mattie asked in an inflated, woozy voice.

This was funny because Coleman's family business, a sports store by the Sound, had collapsed during the recession and he was now, supposedly, destitute and estranged from the wife and kids.

The man reddened and wrenched free his hand, strode on after spluttering out something about manners and breeding.

Mattie burst into laughter. Adrian's teeth were showing.

Eugene said to Mattie, 'You're heartless.'

Mattie snorted at this.

'Comeoncomeon,' Adrian commanded, hurried, and in unison the men sucked down the rest of their drinks – the unmistakable black tilted and morphing to slight crimson and then to yellowed sludge and then to creamy pipping clouds at the bottom of the glass.

The sky was wide and darker. Ahead frost was furry like lichen within the pitted asphalt. An audible pop upon planted foot, another. 'It's baltic, lads,' Eugene shouted, with a fag drooping from his bottom lip. 'Lads?' He cupped his left hand and bent forward. The next pub was Johnny Bloom's. It was up along a further slanted road: Keel always provoked in Eugene this impression of sustained ascension, of conveyor belts. Mattie was blowing blue smoke skyward and he pinched Eugene's arse as he passed. Adrian had powered ahead of the two men – his rollie leaving a glinted trail like foil torn from a lunchtime sandwich – and he swung around now, wagging his head. 'That was nasty, you know,' Adrian pointed at his brother. 'Coleman's not a bad fella.'

The cigarette caught, smouldered, and Eugene inhaled deeply.

'You serious?' Mattie said, and his voice carried.

Snowy wreaths on the doors of the surrounding houses, and in their neat terrace windows, the flicker and gleam of fairy lights. Eugene felt possessive gazing in at these windows now, like each was a glimpse of his own house, like he owned each and every tree webbed in twinkling lights, each and every present beneath, each and every room, and that those inside were stealing from him.

Mattie continued, 'It was a joke. Clearly. What are you on about?'

They were in front of each other now, the brothers. 'No. It was nasty,' Adrian said, his tone grave and self-satisfied. His finger was still pointed at Mattie, and Eugene wished it to be withdrawn.

'You are a spiteful prick sometimes,' Adrian said, 'you know that.'

A car rumbled by and the three men stood aside in the margins of the road, blindly saluted.

'Fuck off, will you,' said Mattie.

They walked on in silence for a few seconds. Perhaps ten altogether.

Eugene said to no-one in particular, 'Bloom's is next.'

'Would you ever lighten up?' Mattie said to his brother. 'Calling me a prick, like. How, like?' His hands were in the air, his cigarette like a baton, and he now glared at Eugene, motioned for his judgement. 'It was a bit of craic,' Eugene reasoned. 'In fairness.'

Adrian talked over Eugene, 'Just stop being a prick, Matthew. Is that so hard?' He flicked his rollie into a garden with a sign that read SANTA STOP HERE I BEG.

'It was only some fun,' Eugene said.

There was a small crowd outside Johnny Bloom's, perched atop the picnic table, or swaying in front of it. Footprints went in all directions on the crusted grass before them, and light spilling through Bloom's stained-glass cast indigo and green and ruby diamonds over these footprints. Someone squawked, 'The boys,' and there was a jolt of braying laughter that filled the night sky, but none of the three men reacted.

Growing up, Eugene had witnessed plenty of brawls between the brothers over silly things: a PlayStation controller, football boots, the ownership of a transparent lighter while they smoked in the McNulty turf shed. And there had been silly fights against others, too. Eugene had been the cooing peacemaker, and when he was not, he found himself throwing wild, clumsy punches. What could he remember accurately? Orange blood like topography on teeth, chesty posturing, tops stripped off and veins glowing violet beneath flesh, girls screaming and tugging on arms and wrists and necks – for a while it seemed like these were, if not necessary components for a big night out, then happenstance which could not diminish one. There was shame in retrospect, or at least distaste as the nuances of a fight evaporated, but never in the frenetic moment of a sparking quarrel. There was only comradery at that time. And exhilaration. Maybe it was all stupid, it was certainly stupid, but it had not felt stupid.

'Mattie,' Eugene eventually clapped. 'What's the rule for this shithole?'

Mattie grinning, 'I'm the sheriff.'

They settled on a booth in the corner, slouching onto the worn cushioned seating. They clinked glasses, cheered, and Eugene inhaled that first milky sip. 'They pour it nicely in here,' Eugene remarked to test.

'Always been a decent joint, this place,' Adrian said in agreement, folding his arms, and the men nodded, and it was as if nothing had occurred outside.

But nothing had, really.

Bloom's resembled more a bachelor's hallway than a pub: narrow with linoleum floors and woodchip walls. It was decorated with framed Celtic jerseys – supposedly signed – and various squad photos of AC Island City FC. In the far back, young bucks were playing pool – Eugene heard the occasional rattle of a potted ball – and three girls in clumpy fur-trimmed ski jackets were bunched nearby. In the booth opposite the men, there was a lad in elf ears, fast asleep amid brown cider bottles. A green and red flag was draped over the upside-down spirits at the bar. Eugene's phone buzzed and he peeked at it, ignored it. 'Fuck, are we the creepy old fellas now?' Eugene said then. He thumbed towards the girls in the back. 'Leering at young ones.'

'Well. You are, champ,' Mattie said, and knocked against Eugene. 'A secondary school teacher aka a functioning paedo.'

Eugene managed to say, 'What age was your first girlfriend again?'

Adrian enjoyed both these digs, and cheerfully said, 'How's the teaching anyway, Eugene?' The silky dum-dum of synthesizer sounded overhead, and Paul McCartney spoke about the moon. 'Good, yeah,' Eugene answered. He began tearing apart a beermat. 'No, it's going good. I'm like furniture there, now. I was actually teaching *Kill A Mockingbird* before the break' – he acknowledged Mattie, who declared it a five-star novel – 'and it was nice to see the kids get into it. But obviously, it can be boring, like. It's a job.' Eugene laughed shrilly and Adrian just looked at him, and Eugene didn't expect to talk any further but he did: 'The holidays are class, too as well, but, you know, when you see the kids get excited about something, or wanting to read ahead, it's really nice like, as if you are—' A gunned finger was directed at Eugene. Then another. Adrian slapped the table.

'Down your drink,' Mattie said. 'Now.'

Paul was singing, 'Ding Dong, Ding Dong.'

Unthinkingly, Eugene had held his breath, but now he understood to smile and be swept along. He clutched his pint and after holding it aloft for Mattie to take a photo, brought it to his lips.

The empty glass spun in the centre of the table for a second. Mattie whistled in a show of – Admiration? Friendship? Disgust? Embarrassment? It was friendship. Friendship.

The door opened and bringing with it the cold.

The unmistakeable clip of heels and the men looked up and shyly back down at their hands and drinks.

Then Eugene started to blow through a small circled mouth as if to quell a storm in his stomach, though he felt completely fine. 'Uh-oh,' Adrian said. 'The poor gasúr is feeling it.' Wincing, Eugene now fanned his unsweaty face with a laminated menu listing a selection of toasties. The brothers were laughing and squeezing one another's bodies at random.

Adrian said to Eugene, 'You never could drink.'

Then Eugene shot Adrian point-blank, and so did Mattie.

Eugene spread his arms in the air and Adrian was holding his face, whining, and then through splayed fingers, Adrian winked at Eugene and they both aimed at Mattie, who half-heartedly decried this spiritual bending of rules. It was like Eugene had stepped through a passage and he was younger. Everyone was younger. All night he would play the prop, no bother, if everyone continued to laugh and laugh and laugh.

The brothers drained their pints.

Eugene applauded them.

Glancing over his shoulder, Mattie announced, 'You know we can't leave just yet, lads.' He planted both elbows onto the table and inclined forward. The mood was switched. He indicated for the two men to shuffle nearer, which was not possible in such a squashed booth, so Adrian and Eugene hunched their shoulders as a symbolic gesture. 'Because you seen who waltzed in there, right?'

Eugene heard the coarse thrill in his own voice, 'Who, Mattie? Who? Who?'

Wrinkling his nose, Mattie sniffed the length of two fingers and, upon encountering his fingertips, held them up and grunted, 'The Ex', to the men's loud amusement.

'Ah, no. I'm only messing,' Mattie then said, sadly, shaking his head, and he set off for the bar.

Adrian spoke close to Eugene's ear, 'My brother is a dope, god love him.' He roped his arm around Eugene's neck, and this tender embrace was snug. Firm. Painful, actually. The lad with the elf ears awoke and there was something dried and bitty on the front of his MIAMI IS 24/7 T-shirt. Unsteadily, he wandered out the door, and the men watched him go. 'It's an early jacuzzi for him, Jeff,' Eugene quipped in the style of a football commentator, and Adrian must not have heard this, because he said, 'I was sorry about Sonia, you know. Honestly. Two years is a long stint.' Eugene managed to shrug in response despite the headlock, and Adrian said, 'How you doing about it all?'

This was a change. Or was it a joke? Was there malice hidden? And if so, where was Mattie in all this? There was a silence now that Eugene felt under pressure to undo, lest it invite a monologue from Adrian about Sonia being a sour, haughty bitch, who wasn't even good looking. 'Grand,' Eugene squeaked, and he tried to avoid Adrian's eyes. 'Like. Grand. You know. Grand.'

'I'm doing grand,' Eugene said to Adrian in summary.

Bodies had formed a ring around the horseshoe counter of the bar, and Eugene found Mattie amongst it: his back was to Eugene, his shoulder blades straining through his polo like a pair of discus ready to be flung as he hoisted his wallet for attention. The memory arrived of clambering after Mattie while on his knees and roaring at that tensed back to relax, to stop. It was all so real and vivid to Eugene now, he could picture it again, he could feel the gravel jabbing into the pads of his hands, feel his hips gyrating like a worm as he crawled, but maybe that was simply because not enough air was currently flowing to his brain, as Adrian's hold was really quite tight? Was Eugene hallucinating? There was the lad balled up in the glassy dirt. His face was visible, or a side of it was. The horrific side. And there was Adrian, calmly watching it unfold. Adrian had eventually picked up Eugene, right? The bottle had already exploded against flesh, and from that particularly horrific side of face, red and darker red was bubbling and mixing with ochre.

That had been behind Alice's. That had been Cooney. Eugene had told the whole story to Sonia once, unexpectedly, and she started sobbing halfway through, though she did not know who Cooney was, had not been . introduced to the brothers, so why did she cry so hard and for so long?

Eugene waved his hand in front of his eyes to test if he was conscious.

'What are you doing?' Adrian asked.

'I've moved on,' Eugene blurted. 'From Sonia.'

'Really?' Adrian said, not disguising his surprise, and Eugene reached for his drink – a movement which meant Adrian had to finally take back his arm – but the drink was all gone, Eugene forgot about that, and so he pressed the empty glass against his soft chin, produced a snobbish scholarly expression to suggest this is what he always intended to do, as he described this new girl he had been seeing – blondie, real nice, fucking gorgeous. He had met a woman for a coffee recently, so it was not a total lie. But the next bit was, 'I snuck her into the school a night there before.' Adrian's mouth dropped open and Eugene explained to it how he had escorted her – this blondie gorgeous woman who did not have a name – through the side gates and in via the study hall and to his desk where he had received – weighing up in his mind that full blown sex was too ludicrous – a blowjob.

Adrian interrupted: 'Head girl, or what?'

They broke into hysterics, tumbled from one another in the booth, and Eugene felt cool relief like a surefooted landing from a marginally perilous height. Mattie returned with three glasses in a single pincer grip and he started laughing too as he shoved the glasses in front of the men – blackish-purple concoctions, a pungent whiff of salt. 'Listen to this,' Adrian said. More were entering the pub, their faces blushing. Aftershave, spent cigarettes, dewy flowers. 'Poxy bastard,' Mattie cried with a huge smile, and Adrian had to say his head girl gag three times before Mattie verbally appreciated it.

'To your one and only blowjob, so,' Mattie toasted, and you had to laugh.

The men supped and stayed on the topic of women. There were graphic reviews followed by intimate insults over mishaps, misdeeds. The fever of packed bodies enclosed them, and it was clammy and horrible in a way, but it was also pleasurable because they decided to be trapped within it. The tables and booths were full. Voices droned along to the music. When had this dump become popular? Time was falling faster, and Eugene realised anticipation was dust: here it all was now. 'Shut up,' Mattie was saying, 'she's still here like, she's going to say hi.' The huge smile once more.

'I love you, Kitty,' Adrian repeated in a cartoony falsetto imitation of Mattie.

And, as though Mattie had been caught in a monstrous lie and global conspiracy, Eugene said to him with a raised finger, 'You did love her though, man. No denying it. You did.'

Mattie shushed them both by calling out, 'Here they are.' Five women were gathered before their booth, cradling goblets tinkling with ice cubes. Adrian was up now, too – bonking his knee against the table as he skidded out. A muffled C-word. Eugene recognised a couple of the glossy faces: Karen Louise who he had kissed at a teenage disco, Hannah Goold who he had fancied throughout secondary school to no avail or embarrassing disaster. Mattie shouted his name. The woman beside Mattie tossed her hair and then Eugene wondered how he had managed to miss her. It was Katherine Kilbane – an old girlfriend of Mattie's. The old girlfriend. A memory of discovering her waspy hair braided into the backseat of Adrian's car, and inserting a coiling string of it into his mouth. She was pretty then; pretty now in a leather jacket with too many zippers.

Eugene loved her. Wow. This realisation like a flash flood. He was always in love with Katherine and not Sonia and it was overwhelming. His mouth ran dry.

Wait, no.

He wasn't in love with Katherine, at all. They had never got on. They had clashed over everything.

Eugene was on his feet and wiping his hand on his jeans as Katherine asked how he was keeping. 'Brill,' Eugene answered, and Katherine eyes widened, and she said, 'Fabulous'. Mattie told a story involving the three of them camping on some beach and torrid rain and a psycho cow and Eugene was certain he was not present for this, but he joined in with pantomime reactions regardless. 'She's a teacher now, too, Eug,' Mattie said, abruptly. The noise of other conversations, and Eugene leaned in to hear Katherine say something about a masters and then Mattie was speaking in a menacing tone, 'You were always a secret swot, Kitty.'

Katherine's brow furrowed.

Should Eugene be privy to this chatter? Should he walk away, walk outside and into the sea?

Katherine said, 'You're doing the twelve pubs? Will you not be rotten?'

Adrian was beside them now, wearing his bomber jacket. He greeted Katherine briskly. 'Show her your jumper, Eugene,' Mattie said, ignoring his brother's arrival, and Eugene did as he was told – he pressed the button in the sleeve and the Santa drinking the beer was lit up by green and red dots. The four of them stared at the jumper.

'Oh,' Katherine said, and she signalled to the other women who had slipped into the vacated booth. 'Well. It was lovely to see you guys,' Katherine said, and she smiled at the men one by one.

'We not having another here?' Mattie barked, and Adrian told his brother no with a vague little laugh. Without a further word, Adrian began to steer Eugene towards the door, his hands clamped on Eugene's shoulders like it was Eugene's confirmation, or as if Eugene was very troubled and ill, and only at the threshold did Adrian reply to Mattie's pleading by calling back: 'Goodbye, my brother.'

They were at the crossroad – right would swing them to the main strip of the town, left was down to the beach and the grassy dunes and playground – and the measly two-tone Christmas lights were guiding them towards the sixth pub: The Sea Shack. The lights were stapled haphazardly across electricity poles: silver and white blubs with an occasional square frame of bulbs, and Eugene was peering at such a dazzling square now, which depicted a sleigh and two reindeers. He said to Adrian, 'Why is there no Santa? Should there not be a Santa driving that yoke? The sleigh thing.' Adrian did not look up and said, far too simply, 'You're mouldy, bud.' Outside the pub, Eugene had asked should they not wait, and Adrian had said fuck him. It was colder. The air prickly when first inhaled. Frost enveloped hedges as if there lurked some colossal spider. 'You didn't have to be so rude,' a voice roared, and Eugene turned, squinted for it. Mattie was loping towards them, headdown, but Adrian and Eugene did not stall or slow, they kept their pace, and, finally, Mattie was wheezing alongside the two men. The Santa hat was missing. Eugene said, 'She released you,' and Adrian shouted, 'Watch your balls,' and feinted to pummel his brother in the groin. Mattie smirked contentedly at this abuse.

After a short distance, Mattie said to Eugene, 'Katherine is looking well, though, isn't she?'

There was Hurley's chipper, and it was hectic. A reek of vinegar from perspiring brown bags, a man using a public bin as a dining table for his chips dunked in pigeon-shit garlic. Smashed glass twinkled here and there on the footpath. Or that could be ice? 'The things I got up to with her in my brother's shitty car, though,' Mattie said, and bumped his shoulder into Eugene's. 'Katherine.'

'Lethal,' Mattie said. 'Mad shit. Insane. Wild. Nuts. Mental stuff altogether.'

This didn't sound remotely sexual or erotic anymore, and Eugene asked in a whisper, 'What did ye do?' Loudly, Adrian inquired if anyone wanted to piss, and Mattie said he might. After the brothers relieved themselves behind Centra, the men took a shortcut up through a sloping back garden and reached the rear of The Sea Shack. They decided to rest and have a fag, stood against the unplastered cinderblocks between the bins and stacked bottles. In front of them were the varying night-shades of the Island: the distinct blued darkness of the roiling Atlantic, the charcoal structures of Keel amongst the irregular pools of orange streetlight, the flattened black of the widest sky and the sleeping Glon. And now the three men were singing mostly the chorus of 'Red Is The Rose'. Followed by Adrian crooning a solo – 'The Bull of West Clare' – with his eyes shut and Eugene was convinced Adrian was about to burst into tears. Then there was an amiable silence for a minute, two minutes, three, when the men only blew out smoke and shifted their weight when muscles began to gnaw and crick.

Eugene trotted on his cigarette, scattering ashy confetti, and spoke, 'It's not a bad old spot, really.'

'When it's not shitting rain, maybe,' Adrian jeered, but it was the wrong space for such a retort, and he went, apologetically, 'But it's home, isn't it?'

Adrian hiked his jeans and answered his own rhetorical question, 'It is home.'

The dancefloor was jammed: couples pressed together and handholding women and ruddy cheeked bucks playfully tussling with other bucks as they encircled the handholding women. Mattie yelled in Eugene's ear: No curse words. They then hugged. There was a thumping somewhere inside Eugene's head and Adrian was giving out to him about roads. Backroads particularly. The absolute state of them. Now he was on about Mourinho being an awful man-manager and did Eugene agree or not and they were still waiting for their stout to be suffused with its topmost layer of cream. A fan loomed over the bar workers, who darted between taps like swatted-at flies. Tacked on the walls were plastic snowmen in top hats – Eugene touched one, the brittle cheapness between thumb and forefinger – and bunting displaying a series of haloed figures pertaining to the immaculate conception, or was it an energy drink campaign? Now they were by a turf fire, pints set on an oval table with an embossed nautical map, and it was much brighter here. Chipped plaster was sprinkled about the stone floor. Nets and ensnared, mildewed lobsters hung down from the ceiling. There was a shiny Christmas tree. Eugene's phone was increasingly itchy in his pocket. It had buzzed again. Beside him, Adrian took a drink and half absorbed a burp and plonked the pint back on the table and then checked and rechecked that it was totally secure on the table. 'I fingered a bird in here before,' Mattie said sagely, and Eugene nodded and thought he should just keep nodding.

'Love to the boys,' Mattie said, and they all kissed glasses.

Eugene licked froth from his top lip, blinked down into his pint: the white that was not quite white, more like snow that had been excitedly pissed on; the ink looming beneath this like a Lovecraftian seascape. Flavour had ceased to exist. Drinking was sheer endurance now. It was a job.

Eugene swallowed some more.

Often, Eugene felt the tremendous pressure that was crushing down his head and brain even when he was not alone and knowingly broken – this scorching-hot, sticky pressure, like two steaming kettles pushing either side of his temples. He would feel it in class as the kids transcribed notes on dead poets, in Lidl as he tossed meals into his basket, in bed at night.

He was feeling it now, actually.

'By the way,' Mattie said, and he stretched out in his walnut captain's chair until his legs crossed at the ankles. He clinched his hands behind his head and winked. 'Katherine will be popping up to us, soon enough.'

Adrian rolled his eyes at Eugene. 'Classic,' Adrian said to Mattie. A deeper breath from Adrian. 'Actually. Classic.'

In response, Mattie tickled his brother's belly, and Eugene was automatically giggling at this when he said, 'It is our lad's night, though.'

To which Mattie frowned and replied, 'How old are you now, Eugene? And you're still scared of girls?'

Adrian told his brother to shut up, and Eugene tried to laugh.

A new group barged into the pub, caused a stir, and, chuckling darkly, Mattie lifted himself from his chair, but was disappointed, and it was twenty past nine and now it was ten minutes later and the brothers were comparing the price of every jug of booze available here with what its contemporaries' price would be in the States. Eugene was making astonished faces to supplement these comparisons. He had not spoken aloud since, but he was making faces. Eugene feared the night's reserve of easy-peasy laughter had leaked, that the stout slump had already begun, and it would be like this now for the remaining six pubs – slurred but pensive discussions about the rip-off nature of drink and petrol and tyres – and Eugene should be the one to mend this leak. This notion struck him, surprised him, as he tugged down his cheeks in reaction to the cost per gallon of whiskey in Ohio. He should bring back the laughs. Wasn't he the prop? The whoopie cushion? The banana skin? 'I want to speak to you two from the heart, my heart,' Eugene said suddenly, and he hiccupped into a fist. 'Listen, listen to me.'

The brothers gaped up at him, their foreheads lined with concern, or maybe irritation, but either way, Eugene knew he was basically invincible – for it is poor form to attack someone so sloppily earnest.

'It's lovely to have you back with us,' Eugene continued, 'to have you home. Even though.' Eugene spoke with what he assumed was a dignified air, like a poet reciting an elegy for a melancholic bog, or a lovely brown-watered weir, or a long-haired, long-nosed woman who had informed the poet that he was the single most defeatist man she had ever encountered in her life.

'Even though,' Eugene said, with a showman grin, a sweep of arm, 'even though, you are two right miserable cun—'

Eugene stopped himself.

'I didn't,' Eugene cried.

Thunderous laughter, flailing limbs, and Adrian labelled Eugene useless. Stone-cold useless.

Adrian turned to his brother, 'He can't drink, I said it a million times. And I'm not minding him.'

'I didn't say it fully,' Eugene said, explained, and he was standing. 'It doesn't count. Please.' Had he been standing for the entire routine? 'I never do anything right, lads,' he said, louder than he expected for he expected this to stay inside his skull. Mattie yanked at Eugene's jumper, pulled Eugene down, and said, 'Imagine this drunkard teaching your kids?'

And, as if it was the reason he was standing in the first place, Eugene exclaimed, 'Toilet.'

In the bathroom mirror, he stuck out his tongue and tried to calculate how drunk he was. When he had positioned an arm steady above the urinal trough, heard the inconsistent thudding of his urine against stainless-steel, he arrived at his conclusion: very, very drunk. A churning in his stomach as he zipped and belted, which Eugene could not name, but which he concluded must be joy. It must be joy, though he had tasted joy before, and it was different: this was rough and stodgy and seemed to be located in his bowels, whereas the joy with Sonia was like a light blanket on a hot, breezy, nakedy summer eve and there was no suggestion of constipation at all. He petted his left pocket and now right. It was actually respectable to be this drunk. He thought he had discovered a secret – in Sonia and the rented house and their accumulation of habits and funny instances to revert back to when glum and in the fog – and it was a secret he felt he should tell no-one about in case they snatched it from him, or dashed away its specialness. But then it had unravelled, it was all squandered. Had he given up on finding that secret again? Eugene was now sitting on a wet toilet seat. He remembered a question Sonia had posed to him on their first day not spent unpacking in the semi-detached house, a question which he had no clue how to answer correctly: What do you want to receive from life?

Eugene closed his eyes. All Sonia wanted from life was a dog and her own little home and possibly a Land Rover. Light fell in bars through the blinds and Sonia had said into his neck: What about you? Eugene's eyes were heavy, so he closed them.

His first text read: I miss you . The next read: I really do . I miss you. The third was his GPS location, which seemed quite ambitious to Eugene even in his present condition.

He scrolled through Facebook.

The fourth message read: did you delete me on facebook? Whats wrong. After everything we did???

Finally he replied to his mother's numerous texts: I'm OK. Having fun and forgot to check phone. Don't worry. Have key xx Go to bed xx Eugene Masterson

He examined the mirror once more before leaving the bathroom, and as he crabwalked past wiggling bodies, he recalled a time when he was hammered after a bottle – or had he gobbled down something bold? And was surfing through the aftereffects of something bold? – and had asked the brothers – dead serious, weepy, nineteen years old – if he was ugly, and the brothers had consoled, No, man, no, no, no, not at all. You're not at all, man. You're good looking as fuck. You're unreal. This is what his mother, and Sonia, and all the others could not see or understand. How did the brothers drag him down? And if they did drag him down, wasn't it nice and warm to be dragged along by somebody? Eugene halted by the exit to the outdoor smoking area. Where were the brothers?

They were gone, they had abandoned him.

Oh. They were in the exact same spot; he could see them when a pair of smoochers spun sideways. Adrian seemed to be inspecting the base of his pint for a fault, while Mattie was craning his neck and absently staring at the entrance. They were not talking to one another, more or less didn't appear aware of the other's existence, and it was dreamy looking over. A vision from his youth. Eugene almost expected to see himself manoeuvring into the scene: a baby-blue Abercrombie shirt with the top four buttons undone, puka shell necklace, blonde tips flecked through his hair, baggy jeans with a long, floppy cloth belt and a hole at the knee that his mother had ripped for him with a steak knife. Eugene was beginning to ask himself would he go back to those days, but the answer was so obvious, so evident, that he started to choke and laugh. What soul would not return to those days? And it didn't need to be the distant past. Probably Eugene would rerun last week if given the choice. Fuck it: he'd take being transported to an hour ago. Anything for a break. He rested an arm against a cigarette machine, which glowed in blurry golds and reds, and continued to observe the brothers not talk to one another from across the room. It was intoxicating. Or he was intoxicated. Both. It could be both. He was hugging the cigarette machine at this point, head tilted on its dusty wood veneer. He closed his eyes again. The music said to Eugene that two thousand miles was very far. He agreed with that. It was for sure.

'Move, or you will be thrown out.'

It was Sonia. She had come to rescue him. It was remarkable, magical. Unbelievable.

Eugene opened his eyes and there was a stranger in front of him with a tower of dripping glasses. 'I won't say it again,' she said through teeth.

Eugene moved. He apologised to this stranger, apologised some more while providing her extra unrequested space by retreating into the carpeted doorway that lead out to the smoking area, where, he now remembered while cowering on the sopping carpet, there was a bolted gate that opened onto an alley that looped back out onto the main street. Eugene could ease himself through this gate and alley and head home after maybe a detour to the beach. Maybe get some chips and eat them by the sea before definitely hailing a taxi. Alternatively, he could skip the chips and head immediately to the sea and watch the waves and then order a taxi, probably order a taxi. The brothers wouldn't mind. They were having a ball without him. Plus, it was pretty much over. The night was pretty much over. I'm going to do just that, Eugene thought. I'm going to leave right this instant.

Eugene parked himself beside Adrian, who groped his thigh affectionately. The brothers had about half remaining in their pints. Maybe less. Eugene had only begun his.

'You get sick, yeah?' Adrian asked.

The dancefloor seemed busier. Noisier.

'Eugene puked his ring up,' Adrian said to his brother, and Mattie returned a thumbs-up.

There was no cheating, no big huge mountain-sized lies. It came out of nowhere. Sonia suggested therapy, and a week later she had her belongings in a carry-on case.

Eugene had stopped treating her like a real living person, this is what Sonia had said to him anyhow. Eugene had once told Sonia she was nothing more than a cleaner. That wasn't polite, probably dehumanising, but hardly enough to justify such an unflattering claim? Except, in general, he had kind of stopped being nice to her, alright. Hadn't he called her an imbecile, a philistine, because she didn't prefer the extended *Lord of The Rings* films? Hadn't he knocked over her vase of flowers because they were in the way of his manbag on a rushing Tuesday morning? Hadn't he avoided meeting her sister? Hadn't it seized him in bumper traffic that he no longer confirmed the hot water was on – a five-second task – before leaving for work? Maybe it hadn't come out of nowhere.

'Katherine hasn't arrived up, anyway,' Eugene said to Mattie, and Eugene wasn't fully sure if his tone was sardonic or genuine.

Adrian let out a phlegmy sound.

'She hasn't,' Mattie said. 'No.' His torso was twisted towards the doorway.

'Women,' Eugene scoffed, and he went to elbow Adrian in the kidney but missed and jutted into the table. Eugene said sorry to the table.

Mattie sighed. 'She said she would join us, I don't get it. That's what she said to me. "I'll join ye". Her exact words.' He was sombre. He was serious. Eugene felt bad. Swishing his glass, Mattie turned to face the men – were his eyes wet? – and confided, 'I always thought she was the one, you know.'

This roused Adrian, who said, 'You went out with that girl for six months when you were in Leaving Cert?'

Eugene decided to start laughing. It was confusing what was going on – had Eugene planned to set this abuse into motion? If so, was he responsible for peppering it with additional comic detail? And, hold on, was Mattie sincerely upset over Katherine? Or was he in on the bit? – but it was good to laugh. It felt good.

'It was a year,' Mattie replied after a period.

'Eight months max,' Adrian said, which rankled even Eugene.

Mattie did not respond to this. It wasn't difficult to tell that Mattie was in a huff and Eugene thought maybe he should let his arm collide with his drink, or shout a string of expletives, or tell them the truth about Sonia and how life seems both endless and pointless and raise the question about whether they had ever rubbed up against such despairing notions, or forge his way into the centre of the dancefloor and wobble like a small child high on Fanta for the brothers' entertainment. And then Mattie did respond, 'I love her, and we went out for a year solid.'

Adrian was smiling at his brother. A mean little smile with reddening cheeks. Now Adrian said, slowly, 'Just because you smashed in some posh boyo's face doesn't mean you love someone, Matthew.'

'Ah, now,' Eugene said.

'Why you bringing that up?' Mattie said.

'Adrian, stop,' Eugene said, and he reached out for Mattie.

Adrian said, 'She wasn't even your girlfriend at the time – that's the funniest thing. Well. The weirdest thing.' Adrian laughed again but it was different, raspy, like unoiled machinery.

'He was cheating on Katherine,' Mattie said. 'He was cheating on her all over the shop.'

'Katherine wanted nothing to do with you at the time,' Adrian said, and clicked his tongue as if puzzling something together, and in this action, Eugene foresaw the sharpened knife: 'And didn't her father call up to our gaff one evening? Didn't he want to have a quiet word with you?'

'Can I not defend Katherine's honour?' Mattie was on his feet, trembling. 'Can I not do that, no? The girl I love. No, I can't do that, I suppose. No.' He paused. 'And you have no idea what her father said to me.'

'Fair point, a very fair and well-argued point,' Eugene said, and pawed at Mattie's wrist, 'but why don't we sit down?' Eugene had his other arm around Adrian, 'Hey, do you remember when I asked you two was I ugly? Do you remember?' Eugene was sniggering to himself. 'What is wrong with me?'

Adrian said, 'You cut apart some young lad's face for the honour of a girl who thought you were a stalker.'

Eugene repeated in a high voice, 'What is wrong with me at all?'

Adrian hummed and looked sideways at Eugene. 'That seems like a completely normal and sane thing for my brother to do, doesn't it?'

'Why you always like this?' Mattie said. 'Picking on me. Putting me down.' Mattie's nostrils flared, and his voice was snotty. 'You love putting me down. Why? Honestly. Why you like this?' Mattie demanded. 'My self-esteem is at rock bottom because of you, and you are meant to be my fucking—'

Eugene said, 'Curse word.'

Eugene's thinking here was that this was an opportunity – perhaps the only opportunity – to infuse levity into such a heated situation. To veer the night back onto the track of steady laughter and fundamentally cuddly abuse and alcohol-based punishment. To subtly avert the night from traumatic confessions. To stop Mattie from breaking down. And before Mattie had him by the throat, Eugene honestly felt his ploy had succeeded.

Eugene's legs were at curious angles: that was where the burning pain stemmed from. His legs. The punch had not hurt, truly, but now there flowered an ache on his jaw, like a thumb-width force pressing down hard, so maybe it did, in fact, hurt a great deal. There were splotches of colours, anyway, primary colours somersaulting through his peripheral vision and now over Mattie's straining face as he leant across and roared at Eugene, 'My self-confidence is fucked.' Eugene was sprawled out on the floor now. The hoofs of the table were right beside his face and he was able to make out an unhealthy amount of loose, feathery hairs and the jagged remnants of crisps. It was gross. A major health and safety violation, surely. Also, Mattie was strangling him a little bit.

Adrian hauled his brother off, and Eugene could breathe once more.

There was commotion above him. The sounds of a scuffle.

The lights on Eugene's jumper were flashing, his collar was torn, and he had no desire to look up, or move at all really, until a bored voice claimed there was a paralyzed man, and someone better call an ambulance. Eugene hobbled up then because that was all he needed.

The brothers were in a meaty heap on the floor and now they were rolling. A nearby table toppled over. The shiny tree next. Glass, as if a rainbow had been smashed by hammer. Plaster was sticking to their clothes like snow. A member of staff watched the brothers with hands on hips. 'What the fuck,' he said to Eugene. There were no punches being thrown. Neither brother was kicking or biting or headbutting. They just rolled and rolled, and occasionally there was a grunt like a revving lawnmower. The reason why they were fighting – though they weren't technically fighting, were they? They were rolling – was no longer apparent to Eugene. Or the reason had begun to lose its significance, was drained of meaningful consequence in Eugene's mind, and so it could be a comic scene if he looked at it in that light. It could be an hilarious incident. Or it could not be happening at all, it could not concern him at all, if he looked instead at the wedged dancefloor, backed away into the thrumming darkness. More staff were over, attempting to separate the brothers, breach their compact ball, and a vast slant of flesh was made visible when a top was roughly adjusted by one of these teenaged workers. The flesh was pale as the moon bar a tawny line of fur, and it was stressed and misshapen, like a pillow stuffed into a school bag. Who did it belong to? They were indistinguishable to Eugene at this point. They were two men rolling around together in a small enclosed area. A bouncer appeared – burly and formidably bald, as all bouncers should be – and in one brutal, professional motion, he had linked his arms around someone's neck and arm – oh, it was Mattie's – and the bouncer was angling this captured arm so that Mattie could easily itch his own shoulder if he wanted to. Together, the bouncer and Mattie wound through the pub like a pair of pissed-up ballroom dancers.

Adrian was on his knees, informing the staff that this wrestling match had nothing to do with him. 'You've the wrong man,' he said.

Eugene was sitting down again. He touched his tongue to his lip and tasted coin. Apparently, he had been clocked a second time. There was damp under his arm and in the linty cove above his arse. He was a small bit dizzy.

'That escalated,' Adrian whispered as he scooched in by Eugene. He was panting and then after some time, breathing in a more level manner. A piece of belly, flab and hair, was on show, and Eugene thought, That is who it belonged to. Adrian smiled, 'Gas enough, though, wasn't it?' and the words sounded broken to Eugene. The phrasing wrong, poorly translated. Something like that was why Eugene didn't respond. Why he chose not to.

Adrian finished his pint and then took up his brother's.

Eugene remembered to drink, and the liquid tasted old and rubbery.

'Sorry,' Adrian said.

'And Mattie is sorry, too. He told me, so,' Adrian said. 'While we were on the floor there. He said he was sorry about hitting you.'

A lad was combing through the broken glass and smashed-up baubles.

'I never got that blowjob,' Eugene said. 'The one in the classroom. That never happened.'

Adrian caught his eye. 'I figured that,' he said. 'It's fine.'

'But I am over Sonia.'

'I'm sure you are'

The bouncer was ploughing his way back towards the two men. 'That's me,' Adrian said to Eugene like it was his bus huffing to a stop before them. He shifted in his seat, necked his brother's pint. 'Come on. We'll see where Matthew's at.'

Eugene held up his own pint: a quarter of stale stout sloshed bashfully. 'I have a bit to go yet.' Eugene hesitated. 'Actually. I'll just leave this, I won't finish it?'

Adrian said, 'I don't care.'

The bouncer was standing over them, and Adrian put his arms up. 'Don't touch, boss,' he said, 'I'm leaving.' Only now did Adrian fix his jumper, cover his stomach. 'Don't touch me,' Adrian repeated, though the bouncer was not touching him.

Outside, Mattie was pacing in a wobbly line. The two men called his name as though it was a surprise party, and Mattie called back their names. The men rushed together and touched one another, yelling excitedly. The sea was to the faraway left, mantled behind chimneys and pointy roofs, its sound faintly discernible to Eugene over the rabble of other parties of men and women, over his own happy whoops. It was comforting to know it was there and Eugene felt certain he would look at it later. The sea. It would be freezing, and only noise in the sludgy darkness, but it would be so lovely still. If he wasn't flopped and drooling over a toilet bowl, he would descend the steep roads and traverse the grassy dunes and look at the sea. If he wasn't hitchhiking home with the brothers, or playing along with them in the pretence of hitchhiking to ward off the misery of walking home in the cold dead night, he would go down and watch the sea for hours and hours. Sit on the beach with knees tucked under chin. Hear the sea crash. Feel it bead against his face. But if worse comes to worst, Eugene thought, Eugene told himself, he could go tomorrow. Head to the sea tomorrow. Scab a lift off his mother or father, no, ask his mother and father to head down with him. With exaggerated thrusts, Mattie was shaking his brother's hand and saying, 'We are sorry, Eug. Look at us. Two sorry boys.' Adrian mentioned the next pub – Flattery's – and what about a rule like no fist-fighting. An objectively terrible joke, but Eugene was laughing, and from a well within himself, Eugene was now retelling what had gone on inside. The knocked over table and Christmas tree. The scared-shitless workers. The pretty women cheering.

The bulging gut on Adrian. Mattie punching Eugene in a friendly, good craic kind of way. How hysterical it all was. Shoulder to shoulder, the men were marching upward. The next pub wasn't but a spit away.

# Bury It

Ada listened. To his whining, his claws as they hacked in furious bursts at the splintered door. The stable was hollow, and these sounds came to her as intimate things. She knew there was no reason to head out to him, that scolding or smacking would do no good. Only agitate, turn the scut that bit more desperate. She kicked a leg from under the blanket, rolled from one side of the bed to the other. It was about twelve. She still wasn't anyways tired. From the bay window, the moon's zincky light drifted in, stencilling her shadow and the shadows of the wardrobe and dresser and the stacked-up boxes onto the cool plaster wall. For a moment, Ada engrossed herself in these coaly shapes and humps, how they settled clothlike on the wall, how they could quickly, ominously shift in length. She ran her nails from her neck to her chest, then at the inside of her wrist.

She should go out to him. She should get up and go out to him. Then she just shut her eyes and listened.

The sheepdog gave in at half three, a hoarse bark his final objection. Ada left her cot only once during the night, to fill her glass of water and stare out the kitchen window. At the overgrown tangle of shrub and nettle and thorn, at the dark blue stable outlined in moonlight.

The evening before, after their walk, she led the sheepdog to the rickety tap at the side of the house. She wrenched it on, hearing the pipes clank and rattle, and stepped back when the water spat out in fat gushes. She rubbed her hands clean and watched his tongue slap in and out. Once satisfied, he smacked his lips, peeked at her and began strolling towards the front door, ruffling his snout from side to side. She whistled. The dog tilted his head. He was old now, with frost jutting like static through his black coat, and firmly grooved into routine. She whistled again, clicked her fingers. Without waiting, she moved steadily round to the back of the house.

The stable was the last skeletal evidence of the tenants who had once farmed this land, before they hedged their bets on coffin ships. It was newly roofed with slanted metal sheets, but its white paint was mottled, flaking like dried skin, and showed its disrepair. Inside there was the everlasting musk of hay, a laddered upper section, and high on the right wall a slit window that let in a scrawny shaft of light. *Rustic charm* was how the estate agent had put it to them three years ago, and Murray had lapped it up. It was the sort of damp authenticity he coveted. Ada was too soft, too easily blown along by his enthusiasm, she knew all this, and yet still she agreed to buy the house and land, though she harboured doubts that it was too isolated, the house too cramped, that they had no real clue of what they were getting themselves into.

Murray had, more or less, finalised the purchase the same afternoon as their first visit, and in the evening, after one too many fiery whiskeys, he drove them back to the house. They hopped the gate, sniggered along the wonkily fenced perimeter of the fields and, with cupped hands, peered through each murky pane of glass – blindly pointing out where they'd put the bookcase, the dining table, the couch. They talked renovations – maybe a new porch, new windows certainly. Where visitors would stay. On the return trek to the car, Murray kept blabbering about how set the two of them were now, that the good times were all ahead, and she had tried not to wonder about what age he thought they were. Murray had discovered his Eden in this gunky soil and its hardy, black-faced sheep, in the scabbing wind and rain, and therefore, in his mind, she simply must have, too.

And there was a semblance of truth in that. Because Ada did craft a quiet happiness within his larger, busier happiness. Didn't she? A routine. The juicy smell of cut grass. The stillness. The sheeted hay laid out on fields studded with rock, the pyramids of turf piled along copper-brown bogs with their sliced avenues. She now treasured those first June evenings in the house, when the sky was the weakest violet and daily tasks had been completed and he'd march out to the stable with a mug, the dog slithering behind, to tinker with his bits and bobs. From the kitchen window, she could see the dog nuzzling and licking its paws, and the reflection of Murray's lantern against the red wooden door. For hours then, she'd be alone in the bungalow, reading or on the phone or flicking aimlessly through the telly, but inevitably she would find herself returning to the kitchen window, to make sure the shine bounced off the red door, that the dog's eyes glinted below like oil on burnt asphalt.

In the three months since his death, she hadn't set foot in the stable. There was no need. Murray's brother, Emmet, had a root around after the funeral and shifted anything of value. Tidied away the rest. 'Piled with crap,' he said, supping his coffee afterward. 'Piled with useless crap. Typical of him, really. Did you know he had a fridge in there?'

Now, as she entered, she realised how shoddy a job Emmet had done. It was cluttered with Murray. Everything she wanted tossed was there, preserved. The two mugs on the shelf above the workbench, the scuffed boots and wellingtons that hung from a series of nails, the cushioned stool pushed underneath the bench. She reached back for the door, for the wall and a light switch that never worked. A bad taste in her mouth. Something scampered by her feet and there was an echo. His voice, she thought. It was his voice again, laced with his brand of foolish excitement, telling her about this or that new plan for the lower sodden fields. How it was all coming together.

Overhead, a bird skittishly flapped its wings. Feathers swirled down. The dog barked. Ada watched as the bird flitted for the window. Hearing his voice. Or imagining his voice. What was the difference? It was her right to imagine if she wanted. Finally, it was all coming together, he had said to her.

The sheepdog circled and barked at the bird and barked again.

She kicked the dog hard and he let out a squeak, and she took a breath until she felt a scald on her throat. Concentrate. Concentrate and think only of this. She gathered the coarse blue rope, hung neatly around the top ladder step.

She sang to him, 'Good boy.' Stooping, she noosed one end of the rope, looped it around the dog's neck and then brought the slack rope through the ring-handle of the door, knotting it tight. The sheepdog stayed still throughout; his head cocked to the side.

He wouldn't settle in the stable. She knew better than that. Spoilt for too long, the dog expected the blanket and the nightly graunch of turf fire. You get used to things and become greedy. She had grown used to the night's total silence and could no longer sleep in her sister's. She was used to the smack of wellington outside the front door marking the close of day.

Ada fetched a can of food from the house and slopped its mushy contents onto the stable's stone floor. While the dog was distracted, gobbling, she latched shut the door. A rotting screwdriver acting as the bolt for the hasp and staple lock. The dog scrambled, scratching his paws against the wood. Ada leaned her weight on the door, listened as he whimpered meekly, as the rope sprang and tensed. Her hand curled around the screwdriver as she told him she'd be back in a minute. Good boy, good boy.

She woke at seven. Her eyes blinking to adjust to the glare that slipped through the curtains, whiting the dresser and the drunk dust motes. It was in the morning, when she lay suspended between yesterday and the newday, that she longed for him the most, felt loneliness the most. And in this groggy inbetween, she found she was able to separate certain facts from the present. So, she imagined him in the other room, prowling for his phone and keys. Or tricked herself he was beside her in the bed, behind her: snug and breathing roughly on her neck. Nothing bigger than that. But still, for as long as she could, she'd try to stretch out this blurry inbetween time, these dull charades, not waking fully until she'd hear the bleat for food. Until she had to begin anew. But today she didn't wait and dream. Instead, she quickly rose and wrapped herself in a lilac dressing gown, moved to the kitchen. The heat wasn't set last night so her breath snaked about her like a veil as she hoisted the blind, retrieved the milk. Out of habit, she switched on the radio – twiddling the volume a little higher. Then she tightened her dressing gown and padded to the front door.

It was a pleasant morning. The yolky dandelions were lush and bobbing, the grass now a different kind of green. Birds. The tinny smell of night rain. On the front step, she cuffed her hands behind her back and looked out at the fields. Thirty-nine acres of uneven and now unused land, trout-brown in patches, soggy and like marsh in others. Further to her right, a tractor was coming along the main road. The tired grumble of its engine even from this distance. In the morning sun, the tractor gleamed like a toy, and she recognised it as Séamus O'Boyle, out on his rounds. She watched for a moment and then waved, aware there was no hope of him seeing her.

After dressing and breakfast, she headed out to the sheepdog.

She counted her steps and got to four and a half before he clocked her. Immediately he was savage, shoving his calloused snout under the toothed ends of the door, snorting. Spraying up dust and red paint pigment. She rattled the fastened screwdriver, shouted for him to settle, for God's sake, settle down, and shrugged the screwdriver free from the chain.

He leaped at her, but the pull of the rope choked him backward. He went to howl then but was winded. 'Good enough for you,' she said. He stumbled about in a circle, retching, spittle falling from his mouth, like jewels. She tried to hate him. 'Now, will you settle?' she asked the dog.

She removed the blue rope from his neck. It was slobbery and tattered at random seams from his gnawing. She lay the rope on the workbench. On the bench's raised top, she noted some stray sawdust. Like pencil shavings. She frowned and swept them away, thought, Where could they have come from?

The sheepdog watched her. His tail thumping the gapped stone, his tongue layered with pools of sticky white.

She pointed and the sheepdog scurried out to the yard.

He had died during Sunday lunch. They had driven to Castlebar to return a faulty lamp and have a gawk around the sales. Christmas lights were still strung across mossy rafters. Warnings for ice on the roads. They sorted their business swiftly, bought things they didn't need, and before driving back to the Island, he suggested grub. Obviously, he had a place in mind. A hotel he had been in years back. Clean, he had promised her.

They sat at a corner table. He collected their food from the brass carvery. She ordered drinks from a passing waitress: a glass of white wine, a rockshandy.

They walked north from the brambled ends of her fields to the pebbled beach of Annagh Bay. The way was messy and rutted and not their usual route. It was gloomy despite the hour, with only fleeting sunlight breaking through the roofing trees and hedges. The dog wore no leash – Murray had trained him to heel at a whistle – and as soon as they cut from the road, he dashed ahead to sniff at tracks and raise a squirty leg on anything he could manage.

The beach was a bumpy crescent, separated from flanking fields by partially collapsed barbed-wire poles. It was a maze of streams and pools and pockets of dumped rubbish. At the entrance, the dog slinked back to her side, cowering for effect. 'Go on,' she said, and he rushed to explore and piss on the boulders and the stranded, bubble wrap seaweed. Already his coat was tangled with briars and petals, and soon the lower bushy threads of fur became freckled with grey sand. Invigorated by the sinewy fumes of the water, the dog was wild. He skirted through the froth of the sea, happy out. His tail flapping as he nosed a shiny bin bag. 'Get out of it,' she roared. He glanced at her, guiltily, black lips smiling, before spiralling off. The sun had been snatched up by clouds, the air moist and greasy, and she remembered his delight when Murray used to feign throwing branches into the sea – the dog's maddened barks alongside Murray's own laughter – and she remembered her own delight when Murray carried the dog into the surf for their evening swim. The dog like a pampered baby in his arms, paws folded as though clutching a blanket. Ada shut her eyes. Her mother had died ten years ago, her father soon after, and there wasn't this. Sadness, yes. Buckets of tears and sleepless nights. Even some ghostly conversations. But not this sense of diminishment: lowered horizons, shorter time. It was all gone, or going, and what was she meant to do? What were you meant to do in life, now?

When Ada turned to walk back, she didn't whistle. Rather she kept her head down and hurried, hoping that this time he was ensnared by the waves or caught under the wheel of a meandering tractor. But as she tramped through a muddy laneway, her gait urgent and unsteady, he hopped out from a hedge and faithfully limped up beside her. His wet feet stepping in time with hers, his tail buffing against her leg. When the dog licked her hand, she swiped it away.

Murray sat down with a tray loaded with two plates of food, a bunch of napkins, and a gravy boat. They ate, and occasionally he'd gesture for the salt or gravy. When she felt full, she automatically went to scrape the remaining strings of her chicken onto his plate.

'No. No,' he said, coughing and lowering his chin to wipe his mouth. He fisted his chest, cleared his throat. 'Actually, why don't you get a bag? For the dog. He loves the bits of chicken.'

Those were his last words, and in the months since, they have been a constant murmur in Ada's head. An upending migraine. A hangover. She wanted nothing more than to change them. These silly irresponsible words. Anything else would do as long as he didn't mention the fucking dog last, as long as that was scoured away.

Ada locked him once more in the stable, not rigging the blue rope around his neck this time. She forced the screwdriver back into the makeshift bolt and walked inside.

A voice rambled from the radio and she knocked it off. She flipped through yesterday's paper, the supplements, the free magazine. Binning the papers, she glanced out the kitchen window. She checked her watch, poured out and then refilled the kettle – spilling water on the counter. As the kettle gurgled, her eyes strayed again to the window. She heard, or at least thought she heard, the scratching, his pained crying. She wiped her hands on a tea towel, though they were dry. Then, after a moment, she plucked the cordless phone from the table and went to the front door.

In the neighbouring field, the tractor was now parked. Beside it was Séamus O'Boyle. And he was working – his back was bent as he broke spade into earth, elbows swinging loosely. They had got on, the two men. Séamus was classed as an old-fashioned gentleman on account of him helping Murray sort through the piles of paperwork needed for vaccinating the sheep – Murray was surprised there was such a thing as paperwork in farming. An admission that now seemed crassly ignorant to Ada, rather than comical, a funny story to tell their friends. The farm had drained money, but it didn't matter – Murray had piles of money. And soon, she hoped, it wouldn't matter at all.

She had offered the land to Séamus. Last week he had paced the fields, back to front, with the sheepdog cautiously in his paunchy shadow. Over the front step, he had told her that it was in fine fettle. It was tidy and a credit to himself. God love him. There was an awkwardness then, and Ada had blushed and heard herself laugh a little too loudly: 'Jesus, Séamus,' she said, and she tried to touch the man's arm, 'he'd never let me hear the end of it if he caught you saying that.' Her price was deemed naïve by her brother-in-law, but Séamus said he'd mull it over and inform her within a fortnight. One way or the other.

Now her eyelids were sore from squinting at Séamus's shape, the sun, and so she took a tissue from her pocket and dabbed them. The man had told her he'd arrive in the afternoon. Probably it was too early, but she thumbed in his number anyway.

It beeped five times before he answered. She heard traffic, this compressed airy bustle, and then a voice, gruff and worn: 'Howya.'

'Dan, hello. This is Ada Grealish from out Annagh.' She left space for an acknowledgment and when none arrived, said: 'The lady with the dog.'

'Oh, yeah. I haven't forgotten you,' he said flatly. 'In Newport at the minute.' There was a rev, a clicking sound. 'I'll be up to you around—' He paused, and she heard the slurp of tongue. 'Ah, I say about three-ish.'

'Perfect. Thanks again.'

'Not a bother.'

The line went dead before she could say goodbye.

The kettle hissed and clicked as she walked through the hallway – free of photographs and paintings, and the flowery wallpaper now so ugly and cheap that she wondered how she ever lived with it – to the living room. It was stuffy with the morning's trapped heat and she slid open the window. On the couch, where he used to slap an invitation for the dog, was a folded tartan blanket. Its wool braided with black and white hairs. Last night she had baulked at the idea of touching it, but now she grabbed the blanket. Fiercely, she jammed it into a cardboard box and fumbled with masking tape – awkwardly, finally, sealing the box, crimping the extra three inches of tape. Then she sat on the couch and crossed her legs. The TV was gone, their small library bare. Her eyes misted, and

she bit into the corner of her fist, willing to hear the van
dragging itself up her road.

Ada looked to the heavens and thanked the waitress, placed
the foam container in the crook of her arm, and turned
to see her husband's toppled body. His head was on his
plate, gravy caking his cheek and ear. His knife and fork
had fallen, rather neatly, alongside a napkin and a fleshy
slab of beef. She stood there, stock-still, for what seemed a
ridiculous amount of time. Then she crumbled.

Voices shouted for a doctor, for an ambulance. A
stranger laid her husband on the carpet and pushed and
pushed his chest. Someone held her arm. Blue lights
twinkled through the front window. Twinkling blue lights.
She felt her legs go and was suddenly held up completely by
this someone. The waitress? Murray was plonked shirtless
on a stretcher. His stomach was so pale compared to his
sun-pummelled neck that she wished to cover him. Hide
him. A transparent mask was tightened around his nose
and mouth and there was no fog. Questions were put to
her and she might have answered. From the hotel foyer she
watched him being wheeled out, the foam container held
to her chest as if it was precious.

Four o'clock and she heard the van cresting up the drive,
the belchy huff of it. She should have guessed he'd be late.

At the front door, she folded her arms as he swung the
vehicle to a standstill. The windows were chalked with so
much dust that she could barely make out the silhouette of

the man inside. The rear licence plate was missing. Jumping out, he patted down the crown of his head before slotting on a discoloured Liverpool baseball cap.

Dan Heslin was a bachelor in his fifties. He was a builder, electrician, taxi or plumber, depending. When she rang him, he had asked no questions, only said a date and price. Below his tarry-grey hair, there were the faint linty makings of a unibrow. He was heavy but not fat, and wore an unbuttoned flannel shirt, tanned boots and knee-bald jeans.

He rounded the van, smacking the bonnet. 'A nice day,' he said. From his breast pocket, he prised a withered pack of cigarettes. He extended the box towards her, but she refused with a hand to her mouth. There was a smell of soot. He stood against the van and pinched himself out an orange butt.

'No rain,' she said.

He nodded, 'Not yet, anyway.' He flicked at a lighter. Two, three times before he got a dim metallic spark.

'The dog,' she said.

'Oh, yeah. I hear he's causing you some trouble.'

'Yes. Well, he hasn't been himself recently.' Ada had rehearsed this lie. Recited it. Still a thirst began to coat her throat. She watched as Heslin brought the fidgety lighter close to his mouth. His large left hand like a wattle wall around the flame, his fingertips appearing a sickly jaundice in the glow. 'He's old now and doesn't come when I call him. Growls when I go near his food. Snaps at whoever visits. That sort of thing.'

Heslin gave a single nod and looked at her briefly, then returned his attention to the sky. He let the smoke roll about his mouth and then, with a jutted lower lip, blew upwards. 'They can go like that, the dogs, when they start to get on. Had it happen myself.' He swallowed a cough, then continued, 'They start to feel useless. So, they turn on you. The arm that feeds.' He spat. 'It happens.'

She tucked her arms tighter to her chest. Wondered how does this man live? Where does he wash his clothes? How does he fuck if he fucks at all? 'He was my husband's dog. He could click his fingers and the dog would, you know.' She smiled and gestured hugely and waited for Heslin to react, to appease her, but he didn't. 'I don't have that,' Ada went on, 'the same control. And the last day, this poor child he went for.' Heslin shot out a tuft of smoke, his eyes half shut. Her voice was a strange instrument she played. 'We were out walking the beach, and he just went for this little girl. She must have spooked him or something, I don't know. But I've never seen him like that. And I had no control over him, you see. I was helpless.'

'For the best, so,' Heslin said after a while.

'We were lucky, you know, to get one like him. Very loyal. But there comes a time.' She was unsure if he was listening. If he even cared at all. Who was she lying to? 'And you'd hate to see him bite someone – to do something like that.' For herself, she added loudly, 'I'd hate for him to do something like that.'

Heslin tipped free a clump of ash from his cigarette. 'Right. Well. Let us finish this fag and you can show me to him.' He clasped the cigarette between his thumb and forefinger and took two lippy drags. His chest seizing inward as he devoured the smoke. It was colder but she didn't risk going inside for a jacket. He slumped a little to crush the butt against the wheel of the van. 'Lead the way,' he said to her.

The sheepdog was curled up when they opened the door. Startled, he lurched forward, and sought to sniff at Heslin – this stranger – and was roughly toed away. 'Get,' Heslin said, and his mouth was open as he inspected the stable, the corners then the celling. Without facing her, he asked if she had anything to tie him with. 'Makes it easier,' he explained.

She retrieved the blue rope from the workbench. The sheepdog, after stretching out his hindlegs, was shuffling towards the door. She whistled.

'Good and tight,' Heslin advised from over her shoulder.

She squatted, ignored the jab of pain in her lower back, and twined the rope carefully around his neck. 'Good boy, good boy.' The dog yawned warmly, his inside gums pink with blotches of black.

'And you have a spot to tie him?' Heslin asked.

'There's a washing line around the side of the house.'

'Grand job.' Heslin stepped forward and slapped the dog on the side of the stomach. 'We'll go get it done, so, will we?' he spoke in a playfully high voice, and it was a couple of seconds before Ada realised he was talking to the dog.

The day had grown nasty. Grey clouds were spread low across the sky. The hedgerows were moving as if being frisked. Rain was close. Ada smelled it as she clutched the rope between her palm and thumb. The dog was stiff and kept bumping into her knee as they walked along.

Except for a few coloured clothes pegs, the washing line was naked, and when they neared it, Heslin reached across for the rope. 'I'll do it,' Ada said, and her voice was unexpectedly fierce. 'It's fine. I'm sorry, I'll do it myself.'

Heslin lifted his hands. 'Ah, yeah, no bother.' He regarded her for a moment, and he kind of smiled, but strangely. 'Look, I'll grab the gear. How about that? But do remember to rig it good and tight, yeah?'

She dragged the dog forward and waited until she heard his boots crunch away. Then she twirled the free end of the rope around the pole. 'Good boy.' She went on her knees and there was an unbearable shock up through her back. She held her breath till the pain subsided somewhat, and she felt his gaze intensely. The thought raged: she wasn't strong enough, she needed him and not the other way round. 'Shush.' She knotted together the short ends of the rope. The dog was panting, tongue hanging to one side. Her hands were numb as she fastened the chord. 'Shush. Be quiet, please.'

'How you set?' Heslin called, a duffle bag slung high on his shoulder.

She leaned forward to check that the main line was sturdy and then she tugged at the noose. As she combed her index finger around his neck, the dog's breath was hot on her face. 'One second,' she said. Her hands trembling, she rubbed his chin and snout. She itched his wedge ears and the scraggy white fur along his neck. She struggled to exhale – a stickiness in her throat. The sheepdog whipped her fingers with his tongue.

'OK,' she said, 'OK.'

The duffle bag was dumped at Heslin's feet. He crouched to unzip it. The dog tried to follow her, but the blue rope tightened, and he was restrained. Did he know to chase after? He moaned at her, let out something smaller than a bark, and she tried to ignore the silver and chestnut that probed at the corner of her eye. 'I better go inside,' she said. 'I think, I think that would be for the best.'

Heslin shrugged, 'Whatever suits.'

She hastened to a trot as light beads began to fall. Only once did she allow herself to glance back. There was Heslin, the gun splayed open in his right arm. There was the sheepdog, rigid, watching this encroaching stranger, his tail wagging.

In the waiting room, a doctor questioned as to whether her husband had suffered any chest pains recently. Murray had felt some pins and needles. That's all it amounted to. Pins and needles. The other evening. In his arms, maybe chest. He came in to her and said that. The doctor nodded along as she spoke, and when Ada was finished, or when Ada allowed the doctor the chance to speak, he said that Murray wouldn't have felt a thing. It would have been over before he even knew what was happening. Out like a flash.

This was meant to console her, Ada understood. Meant to grant her the solace of knowing that Murray didn't suspect he was dying. But where exactly was the solace in that knowledge? Wouldn't it be much, much better if you did know you were about to die?

Ten minutes outside of Castlebar, the car swerved into a gravelled layby. A scattering of stones. Her hands bone on the wheel. It was raining mildly, more like sleet in the headlights, and the flat plum-coloured fields and little hills were frozen already, sparkling ever so slightly. There was no noise except the heart-thump of the wipers and the shiny flash of rushing cars. His sunglasses case was in the glove department, his pristine AA road maps were tucked into the door panel, the comfort beads – that he had insisted on buying despite having no back problems – dug into her spine. She started to cry. She pushed her knuckles into her eye sockets, felt tears, and pushed harder and harder and harder.

When she heard the shot – a solid sound that seemed to snip through the air in front of her – she placed a hand to her neck. She did not flinch, she did not scream, and after a moment, she went on with stripping the bedsheets. Working rapidly, she tore the cover out from under the mattress, pulled pillows from their silky case. She packed them away and went into the spare room, began to rummage in the closet, and only stopped when she heard Heslin's fist on the front door.

'All done,' he shouted in.

When she came out, he was smoking, his back to her. Dots were appearing on the windows of his van. 'How did it go?' she asked. She grasped a brown envelope with both hands.

He nodded. 'Quick and easy when it comes down to it.' His shoulders rose and dropped. 'Ah. Not the nicest make of business. But,' he said, and he seemed to be consulting his cigarette, 'there you are.'

The sheepdog lay on the front grass, like a wet lamb pulled prematurely from its mother. The blue rope was around his neck. Eyes were thankfully closed. The only difference, she noticed, was the stream of pinks and bruise-purples that ran along his chest.

'It's finished anyway, and, well,' she said, though she had nothing else to say.

Then she handed him the envelope. Heslin, placing the fag in his mouth, fingered it open and counted. He shoved the envelope into his arse pocket and hitched his neck towards the dog. 'What you want us to do with him?'

Ada led the way, a shovel under her arm. Heslin was two steps behind, dragging along the sheepdog, who was covered in a woven coal bag. The ground underfoot was soft, squelched with water, and the yellow reeds had darkened to filthy green. The tall arrowheads of fir trees rocked from side to side. Rain fell and fell faster in exquisite zips of silver.

In the furthest field she instructed him to dig. He moved a hand to his breast pocket but reconsidered and grabbed for the shovel. He began to cut into the sloppy crust and there was a kind of beauty to his spadework. He sifted through soil and mud and sludge, gouged clean dangling roots and rock, burrowed down while she watched from above.

A round hole was gutted in twenty minutes. 'That'll do.' Heslin planted the shovel in the mangy grass aside the hole and, using it as a sort of banister, hauled himself out. And now the sudden whoosh of a gale and the rain turned at them sideways. Wincing, Heslin sniffed and rejigged his baseball cap and then went to gather the dog from the coal bag. 'Up you come,' he said to it.

He eyed her. 'Want to say anything?'

'Just bury it, will you?' she snapped. She was drenched to the bone. Her tears mismatched with the great deluge of rain.

Heslin trudged to the rim of the hole and, bending one knee, let the sheepdog roll in. Her breath faltered. For a second, she imagined that this sack of flesh might now shatter into a million pieces like a glass bowl, like a china plate, but no. It didn't. Of course, it didn't. The dog only slid slowly down the hole, much slower than she had expected, and then with a dull clunk, it landed. At the top, the blue rope had snagged itself around a dried root. Spotting this, Heslin booted the rope in before wiping his runny nose on a frayed sleeve. 'Right,' he said, and he reached again for the shovel.

# A Short Story

He was the last to emerge from the changing room, a conscious choice, and he was presently deciding, stood as he was at the end of the tiled hallway between the communal showers and swimming pool, how best to disguise his horrific body. His belly, his saggy sandcastle tits. A trick he often used was to adjust his swimming cap as he marched towards the water – fingers tentatively plucking the cherry-coloured latex about his forehead. Or another ruse was to fiddle with the off-white strings on his togs, knotting and then unknotting like it was a right doozy of a puzzle. But considering today, this meeting taped together by unseen texts and unverifiable facts and by the understanding that he would get the shift at some stage, John figured he should garner that first easing laugh from them, from her, by racing, leaping, and bombing into the pool. A gigantic splash and there'd be hoots and cries at this rather than at the doughy spectacle of his body and the lumps which unfolded from it, like sacks hooked to an air balloon carriage. And John could happily snicker along too because he himself had determined to be the joke. He was twelve, almost thirteen, basically thirteen.

John peered out at a large hall decorated by grey statues of topless women holding pots which unloaded streams of water. There was a single deck chair for a lifeguard who was not on duty. Fake plastic ivy haired itself around four columns and encircled the steaming but vacant jacuzzi. Bang in the middle of the pool was Studzy and the two girls, Karen and Niamh. A pale ribbon of disturbance. With his middle finger, John picked at the grout veined between the turquoise tiles on the wall. Heady pool smells: wet coins, disinfectant, spoon-fed medicine. Through the far floor-length glass, the sky was blue, and the sun was bright. They hadn't seen John yet and he didn't want to stare.

Studzy was ducking his head in and out of the water. In profile, it wasn't clear if he was in the middle of talking to the girls and this was some drowning sequence in a story, or he was just amusing himself. Studzy was never publicly constrained, and this made John jealous, though he could not articulate this jealousy to any enlightening standard. Instead, he looked upon his friend's shamelessness, his crass unshyness, as Studzy being thick. Admittedly, annoyingly, Studzy was also brave: bravery meant the ability to yell at girls across the street, in being able to flake a rubber at the back of someone's head during class. John envied this, too, and so he had to blame this obscene courage on the fact that Studzy was poorer and did not own a PlayStation 2 yet. The girls' backs were to John. From their wet hair, sleeked to mulch-brown and black, he could recognise who was who and who was her. No one else had on a cap though a rule in the changing room read PLEASE WEAR A CAP. He really didn't want to stare but there was a diamond of flesh beneath her swimsuit straps. And her skin was sallow there, like the underside of the dining room table. Words came to his mouth, and John couldn't not speak them, so he did, softly: NiamhIrwinNiamhIrwinNiamhIrwin.

It was then he heard his name called.

An immediate clench in his stomach, as if butted by the nub of a hurl, and instinctively, John's elbows aligned with his shoulders. He barrelled forward – a sign declared No Running, and so he did not run – his fingers busily unravelling the strings on his togs. It felt, at that very moment, like the world's spotlight was angled his way, a dusty sulphur highlighting his body and its many problems, and he ordered himself to keep his head down. Not to acknowledge this light. Not to look at her. All he desired was for his tits to flatten like forked-down mash, for his gut to appear moderately normal, for him not to slip and fall and leak apart in front of them, and right by the steps that twisted down into the pool and equalising water, when he thought he had reached safety, when he thought his prayers had been somewhat granted, John heard his surname thinly shrieked.

So close now that he could not feign deafness; he was obliged to look over.

Studzy held a dribbling arm aloft. A smile like he owned too many teeth. He shouted, 'Finally!' John sucked in his stomach till there was a frowning crease in its centre and he saluted his friend by jerking his right elbow even higher. His foot popped into water and from the corner of his eye, John glimpsed the girls, expressionless and watching, and with that glimpse he recalled how sick and frightened and hideous he was. His fingers wrenched the strings on the togs, and despite the water being scarcely calf-deep, John decided now was the time to plunge his body fully in.

He bonked his left knee against the second last step, and it ached.

The embossed tile harsh against his chest.

Bubbles, green-blues, a newspaper rustling sound, sudsy rips of white. Then John began to kick, swim.

He emerged an arm's length from the girls. Far too close, he sensed. Weirdly close. So, he paddled to their left. Against the pool's floor, his feet were comfortably flat, but still he levelled his chin to the water's plopping limit, hunching his shoulders. As a result, his face – a shiny and very round face – was solely on display.

'Well,' he said to Studzy.

He bobbed, groping the back of his knees. The pool tinkled around his ears.

'Hey,' he said to the girls while mostly looking at Studzy.

They replied in musical unison. 'Hi.'

Studzy snorted and whispered nosily to the girls, his left hand elaborately shielding his mouth.

Niamh – the girl who would supposedly kiss John, who supposedly liked John – grimaced at whatever was said. Her lips large. High forehead. And her eyes. A squawk from Karen which she tried and failed to contain with a cupped hand.

Studzy flailed from the girls into a shoddy backstroke, feet squirming in and out of the water. 'What's with the gay hat, like?' His blocky incisors appeared.

To show his indifference to this abuse – though not because he was a sensitive baby spoilsport who couldn't handle a joke, but because he was truly indifferent and because his dad explained you didn't get picked on unless people really, really liked you – John studied the exposed ceiling and did not reply.

Studzy slapped water at him and his laughter stuck in the air.

John liked Niamh's eyes the best. Tiny blue eyes with dolly lashes. The drained blue of a sweet you'd suck on to rid a cough. He would like to be able to study her eyes in say a mirror, as to be tangled in them directly – as he was now, his gaze lowering from the ceiling toward the fog-dappled screen of the sauna and accidently catching hers in the process – wrangled together his innards so he felt fatter and uglier, pricked at what must be his heart. If she had a blemish then John could not see it, though, maybe, her see-through braces. The thing was: he hadn't known he liked Niamh so painfully before Studzy had shared the fact of her liking him a week and a bit ago. After that, everything John had once understood was askew – songs rang differently, Shaggy's 'Angel' was profound with verses of dense resonance; school was pointless; his posture was straighter; he no longer ate with just a fork. On Friday, he had shunned the wheeled-in television and passed through the afternoon by writing her name, again and again and again, on the last page of a copybook. After each upright scrawl, her name grew loftier, queenly, shedding its nominal meaning and gaining something deeper, more spiritual, more mysterious, each letter noiselessly expanding in his mouth and ears and in the reddish murk behind his closed eyes.

Niamh Irwin. Niamh Irwin. Niamh Irwin.

'And what took you so long in there?' Studzy asked now.

Karen laughed again. John disliked her more than anyone alive.

'You gomey,' Studzy went on, swatting towards John. 'Were you taking a poo?' Studzy glanced at the girls and said louder, 'I bet you were taking a massive poo.' On Studzy's left cheek, there was a diagonal gash, a pink fatty scar. When Studzy grinned, as he did now, the gash crinkled and grinned, too. Studzy had never divulged how he had earned this scar, it was hush-hush even during sleepovers, but John had whispered to quieter lads that Studzy's own father had drawn it. One night, his father had prised a poker from the fire and sizzled his initials into his youngest son's cheek. The story was baseless, obviously. There was no hint of lettering in the scar, no evidence of turmoil between Studzy and his family, and, to be honest, Studzy's dad was really nice and funny. Yet John told this story. However, if it was one day tossed wet in front of him, John would deny to the removal of his dick that he had ever conjured up such fiction. Likely, John would sincerely believe he had not made the story up. Studzy was a friend, unquestionably his friend, but John feared him in the manner that you could only fear someone who was intimately wise to you, who was above you in the official standings.

'I wasn't long,' John said and meekly added, 'Fuck off.'

A chesty grunt from Studzy at this. The girls were backed by the light from the glass wall, and John squinted. 'I was only after you, sure.'

Studzy splashed him again. More aggressive this time, a karate chop. 'You were,' he said. 'Ye*aaa*h.'

John replied, 'I was.' Then drawled, 'Ye*aaa*h.'

Studzy giggled and John was comforted by the warm privacy of this gag, in the knowledge that the girls could not understand why it was so hilarious. Together, the boys jostled over this oiled joke for a moment, three, both repeating the punchline in various accents while flattering the other with hearty laughter till the routine was absolutely exhausted. The girls smiled throughout, a coyness in the stretch of their lips as if they hid communion in their mouths. There was silence now, and they all swayed in the pool before Studzy shouted, 'Watch,' and thrashed off into a front crawl.

They watched. His half-closed hands pawed rather than scooped water. There was a great spillage of foam after him. Studzy awkwardly peeked back once, spewing liquid from his mouth, a deranged bloat to his eyes, and then kept going. He definitely never went to lessons, John thought with satisfaction.

Studzy and John became friends in first class because there were sixteen in the class. Their friendship tightened over the years because Studzy was cool and because both were handy at football: Studzy was a skilful corner forward who seemed not to possess a bad foot, while John was a goalkeeper at the age when no one wanted to be the goalkeeper. Last year, while swapping Pokémon cards, Studzy had said John looked like Snorlax – the obese Pokémon – and this was parroted repeatedly by a boy named Joey. John had reddened and hastily packed up his folder of cards and OK, yes, shed a few tears. At big break, Joey was stabbed in the thigh with a protractor by Studzy and then punched by Studzy's brother after school. The name calling ceased.

Gasping, Studzy stood up in the shallow end of the pool, and bellowed, 'I win.' Had there been a race? Water piddled from him in flashes. His navy Adidas shorts were craggy in their sogginess, and why had John failed to point out they were not official swimming togs earlier? Studzy excessively wrinkled his nose and sniffed. The crisp sound of clotted snot, wicker swept against stone. John figured Studzy would spit now and describe exactly its colour and thickness, but instead Studzy swallowed and asked: 'Comehere, Niamh. How's the football going?'

'Good,' Niamh answered, 'it's going good.' Her tone was chirpy, birdish. She didn't look across at Studzy.

'We have our semi-final next Sunday. Our county semi-final.' The four of them were gathered in a rough square. Then Niamh flicked her head. 'You know Karen plays, too, right?'

'Oh, I know, yeah,' Studzy said. He was flustered. Surely, John thought, he should be immune by now to the perils of back and forth conversation with a girl? 'Fair play,' he said to Karen, and he went on, 'Honestly. County semi-final. That's unreal.'

Niamh scrunched a face toward Karen. 'Thanks for the support, Enda,' Karen said. The girls both laughed. Studzy sort of laughed, too.

And it seemed like John was about to speak. There was this gap and it felt like he was shoved forward to say something consequential for the benefit of the group, or at the very least something coherent and worthy of a shrug ('True. The county semi-final is unreal.'), but this tingle receded, like a pinch on the upper arm, and John's tongue just rolled circles in his mouth. Around him the pool stirred and dipped in intervals. Wide drains gulped and gulped hungrily once more. It was quiet, well, the place was empty. Because of the weather? Studzy started telling a story about this time down by the GAA pitch where the two of them – 'me and Johners' – had flung a rock at Miss Quinn's parked car, cracking her front window. Quinn being their principal. Running through the events, Studzy gestured at John – a head tilt, a side-eyed-gawk – and when he did, John nodded and sniggered as if a switch had been flipped on his neck, though not a huge amount of the story was factual. They had thrown a rock, yes, but it had hit the rear wheel not the window. And it wasn't really a rock. More a fistful of gravel which they slung as they hared by the hatchback, steamy and pumped after training. And it wasn't just the two of them either: there had been five in the group and John was the straggler who didn't, in the end, fling his share of gravel, but rather allowed it to sieve down through his half-closed fist. The story was soon laboured with explanation for why such and such was funny, the girls not being familiar with the joys of provoking rallies from authority, nor understanding why Quinn deserved her car to be pelted with rocks in the first place, and it spun to a jarring conclusion: the window was brutally smashed and Miss Quinn was now actually inside the car, howling, and there was a chase from somebody shadowy, a Guard, maybe, possibly, likely, and Studzy had no clear notion how they managed to get away. But they did.

'It was gas,' Studzy said. He pushed at the water with both arms and eddies formed. 'Wasn't it?'

John motioned agreement. At certain angles, it probably was gas.

After a while Karen said, 'She's my neighbour.'

Niamh adjusted a swimsuit strap with the curve of her thumb, flipping it right side up. Her shoulder held a gloss, like frost only melted.

Studzy chuckled. 'Unlucky,' he said to Karen, and chuckled some more.

'As a matter of fact, she's really nice,' Karen proclaimed. 'She helps my mom a lot. Since Dad.' Niamh placed a hand on her friend's arm and then stroked it. John nodded solemnly. Her dad had died in a car-crash. The whole Island knew that.

Studzy mumbled he was sorry.

A vent huffed from somewhere overhead. Along with it, the clucks of unseen pipes.

John should offer a consoling phrase here, too. Sorry your dad is dead. Sorry about your dad dying in that head-on collision out by the Glon. John willed his tongue, wriggled it, but nothing.

This was all Studzy's design. For them to go swimming at the hotel, to meet there on Sunday, to borrow John's free passes. When John questioned, Why the pool? Studzy had simply answered, Do you ever stop being a little bitch? For three weeks Studzy had been texting Karen. And each morning before school since that initial exchange of digits, a crew had formed in the paved backyard, trading ringtones and a wheezing, pocked soccer ball as they waited for Studzy to strut in and reveal whatever had been exchanged between boy and girl the evening before. There was nothing ever raunchy in the texts – nothing that alluded to the anatomy and rules they had learned from dictionary definitions and a robbed booby magazine – rather the messages were fixed around whatever eight o'clock TV show was on and homework and intricately patterned Xs, and on a single teasing occasion, a digression about which of the lads she reckoned was decent. But in these placid texts, John still discovered a tetchy buzz, which made him feel both stressed and thrilled, sweaty and cold. It was like the sensation of being bold when you're normally very good.

Karen kept blinking, her gaze roaming about the hall, and Studzy was talking about how Quinn was sound literally most of the time, well, some of the time, and Niamh, ignoring him, carefully asked Karen was she good? Karen took a deep breath but didn't answer this elegant question. John studied the water. He had not noticed till now the heaviness of the chlorine. He dimly rubbed his right eye with his fist. It then stung. Studzy now muttered something to John but John was unable to comprehend what was being said to him, because, at that exact moment, Niamh was combing her fingers through her hair. Her ponytail was undone – when had that occurred? – and how different was her hair when it was being slowly raked through. The various shades of brown. The black gogo on her wrist. And her small earlobes, he noticed, were pierced with identical studs, silver crescents, anorexic moons, and there was a dark mole on the springy rim of her left ear and.

Studzy hoisted himself atop John's shoulders. An arm was roped around John's neck. There was an elbow, here and there. John slouched under the new weight, yelled and then struggled. 'Got it,' Studzy screamed. The girls were amused, John heard but did not see. The swimming cap flew off, was pitched toward the deep end where it floated on the surface, forlornly, and then it sank, a smudge in the pool, like a murdered bird. John drank water: strangely warm, bad tea. Then he was in the water. Saw the pallid shapes of their legs and the cute bend of her knee, wavy, pixel-like, but oh, so real. Her footnails were painted ruby against the hexagon tiles and John was admiring them when he remembered he needed to breathe. He smashed through the sheet above and his fingers curled around the heels which straddled his neck. John cast Studzy from his shoulders. An explosion. Gleaming white. Water hanging in the air like spooked feathers. Hysterics now. Studzy was laughing. The girls were laughing. And John went further, dunking his friend's head – pushing it down with more violence than he had intended.

Underwater, Studzy wiggled and crawled away.

John watched him drift off, panting a little, feeling invigorated, this ripening urge to howl and cheer and wrestle some more, and only now did he realise his slopes and rotten blubber were plainly, pinkly exposed.

He stooped down.

The girls. Had they seen?

Time reduced to normal, but John was flushed, felt outside it. He held his breath and peeked over at the girls, trying to appear inconspicuous by placing both hands on his forehead, as if checking his temperature. There was no marked change in their faces. No recognisable disgust or mirth or lips wilting to shout, Fatty. Though that only meant, John knew, they were thinking it. That only meant that they would mock him in private later.

'That was funny,' Karen said then to John. 'Do you and Enda fight like that all the time?'

When they shopped together, his mam referred to John as 'broad' to the shop assistant – Well, she'd say, he's a little broad, exaggerating the word, singling it out, you know, broad in the shoulders – and lately, John found he could uncover the implications behind her description, and when alone, he would replay these scenes but with her fraud words replaced: My son is fat, you see, he is a fat arse, he is a fat fuck.

'Amm,' John answered, and Karen pursed her lips at him and then she had dimples. She was encouraging him, John understood that, felt that, and a rush came through him, like a forefinger thrusted down his throat, and he spoke, finally, to the girls, albeit as a single, breathless word, albeit by snubbing Karen's question altogether: 'Whoyouplayinginyoursemifinal?'

Niamh stared at him.

Not meanly, Karen said, 'What did you say?'

But John did not repeat himself. He did not need an answer. He had only wanted to speak.

Studzy sprung up from the water, having played at being drowned without any spectators. He waded sluggishly back towards them.

From the sauna, the fart of escaping heat. An old man hobbled out. John watched him shamble by the length of the pool, glad for the chance to turn. Something important had happened. He had opened his mouth and spoken. The sheer enormity of it. It was like he had saved a certain goal. Wait: Would they be thrown out and banned if they kissed here and now in the pool? Because wasn't that exactly what was about to happen?

He imagined himself and Niamh amid the cumulus bubbles of the jacuzzi. Kissing.

Eyes open and lips kissing and tongues doing whatever they do.

'What was I going to ask?' Studzy announced. The old man deposited himself into the jacuzzi with a baa of contentment. Studzy stretched out both arms, rotating them at the wrist. He clicked his tongue. 'Oh, yeah.' He looked at John and he said, 'You two heading to the disco next weekend?'

The disco was held in the sports hall in Mulranny. It started at half eight and was over by eleven. The black and white posters advertising it read EPIC NIGHT and DRESS TO IMPRESS and in smaller writing Strictly Non-Alcoholic Event. In the centre of the poster was a stippled image of Britney Spears with a python. Upon spying these posters – on the electricity pole by the school, taped onto the front glass of Brett's – John felt oppressed, as if the event was a birthday party he had been told about and subsequently disinvited from. When some of the lads expressed notice of the disco, schemed about tickets and lifts and choreographing breakdancing moves, John felt sure he was going to vomit.

Studzy answered his own question: 'I'm going. Be my second one, like. I went to Christmas Madness in January there.' He batted at his nose with an open palm and then at the water as if it was in his way. 'It was class,' he said.

Karen said that she probably would go. If she could afford a ticket, and if she wasn't at her cousin's in Cork that weekend, and if she didn't have soccer or piano lessons. Some of Niamh's hair had frizzed around the back of her neck, strings, stringy, and it reminded John of grass poking out along the margins of an old road. Then it reminded him more of a lady in the booby magazine and what was so spherical and tantalising within those pages.

He required the ceiling.

'You know, this fella's mam has him banned from discos,' Studzy said.

A beat, a stifled giggle from Karen, and then John clocked this was aimed at him. 'No, she doesn't,' John snapped. Studzy beamed toothily at the girls. 'I haven't even asked yet,' John continued, faster. He was unsure suddenly if he may, in fact, have been banned from the disco. Was Studzy privy to knowledge he was not? John forced a laugh, which clicked hollowly rather than rang out for the girls to hear and acknowledge him as an active and enthusiastic player in the joke. His cheeks were warm. 'I definitely will be going.'

'I definitely will be going,' Studzy mimicked.

Niamh and Karen laughed.

Ignoring this, John asked in Niamh's general direction, 'Will you be heading to the disco yourself?' His cheeks were very warm now, in fact were burning, possibly were melting.

Studzy persisted, 'Well. Your mam didn't let you go last time, did she?'

John shook his head as merrily as he could to demonstrate he was fine with this joke continuing. In on it, actually. 'That was last time. She never said anything about the next one,' John said, and he looked at no one in particular. 'I'm not banned, or anything.' Niamh had not responded, or indicated she had heard his question, and it terrified John that it may have been ignored, silently ridiculed, and was now tainted, sunken. But maybe, John reasoned, she had just not heard it. Perhaps the question had sort of glided over her, uncatchable, like a shanked kick-pass? 'My mam said nothing about the next disco,' John explained and hesitated and then added with slowed authority, 'Seriously: I'm not banned.' The most miserable action John could undertake now was to repeat his question to Niamh. Even if she just hadn't heard, it would still be desperate. It would be sad. He shouldn't do that.

John said to Niamh, 'So, you think you'll probably be heading to the disco, as well?'

'Did you know his mother's a ride?' Studzy spoke over John. Studzy was expectant here, but this was not his usual audience. 'You wouldn't guess it looking at him,' Studzy said, and went to pinch John's tit.

'Stop,' John slapped him off.

'Oh. Trish,' Studzy whined, and he tried for the nipple once more.

Another slap from John, then a badly directed fist, and, cackling, using the girls as a shield, Studzy escaped. He cawed John's mam's name again – elongated to a masterly extent – and it was accompanied by a middle finger gamely entering a hole fashioned by Studzy's thumb and index. Karen told Studzy he was disgusting. Trish rebounded above – a sound that did not seem to be fading, seemed to be growing louder – and John wanted to catch his friend, pummel his friend's face in, strangle his friend, kill his friend, but was motionless. Now Studzy licked his bottom lip and let out a sex noise, or what their class had unanimously agreed was a most likely sex noise: a guttural goosehonk followed by a drawn-out, exhausted whimper.

There was a short silence before Niamh faced John. 'Nope,' she said simply to him, 'I haven't *permission* to go to the disco.' Her mom, the fool, had freaked at the idea of her going before she was in first year. It was really, really unfair. Totally unfair. John's head nodded along to each delicate syllable of this explanation, and when it seemed Niamh was finished speaking, all he could manage was, 'That's so cool.'

Then John corrected himself, 'I mean, that's so annoying.'

'We could sneak out,' Karen said to Niamh, who narrowed her eyes. They slid from John, squeaking together, and as they sailed away, John pictured himself as a dog being shooed from a plate of food.

But it was a nice shooing.

Sort of exciting, honestly.

His hat soared through the air and splattered before him. Big laughs from the girls and John smiled and reached for it.

This was a wonderfully considerate gesture, too.

From across the pool, Studzy called out, 'Talking about football, Johners.' John looked over, startled, and Studzy went, 'Are you training tomorrow evening with the Under Thirteen's?'

Despite lifts being arranged between their mams, despite Studzy being informed to be stood outside his estate no later than five-twenty-five, he asked this now.

It was difficult to know if Studzy was genuine here. It was equally difficult for John to know if he was being genuine when, in reply, he thought not to answer the question but, rather, to methodically examine the entire notion of football training, as though it was a concept that had just cropped up in either of their lives. John elaborated on the negatives of training with the older lads (the excessive running, the dickhead manager and his whistle, the older lads) and the positives (smacking a ball, the small game at the end, the honour of being deemed class enough to play for the age-bracket above one's own) and he concluded, after a thoughtful shrug, that he will train. May as well, like. He said to Studzy in a sort of shout, basically shouted at Studzy, 'I can probably collect you for our training with the Under Thirteen's tomorrow evening?'

The girls were in the deep end, a hand each on the wet edging tile. The outline of their gently kicking legs could be seen through the water, a tad disembodied from their torso. The colour and sparkle of white stone, quartz. Had they heard? Were they seriously impressed?

Studzy nodded at John, appeared to be weighing up this offer of a lift – though he had already agreed to it, hadn't he? – and then Studzy completely swerved course and mentioned the blazing sun and mused about whether they should not head uptown for a bit? 'All four of us,' he said, and he surfed nearer to John. The girls did not say anything but were looking over. 'Maybe we head up to the playground?' Studzy suggested, and he raised both hands, 'Or a spot like that. The playground is decent enough, actually? I don't know.' There was a pause. The wrong-channel hiss of the pool. The hands splashed down. 'But how about we all go to the playground?'

The girls agreed.

Was that supposed to happen?

'Let's leave, so,' Karen challenged. She was swimming back to them.

Studzy said, 'Deadly. Cool.' There was an archness to his voice. Already, he was unbalanced by his own invitation.

John clutched his tits underwater and tried to smile. He was aware, far too aware, he was the one nearest to the looped steps which exited the pool and by common law, he should be the one to stagger out first. 'So, we wander uptown.' John heard himself squawk out these words. For what reason, he did not know. Luckily no one heard him. He decided to believe no one had heard him.

Karen said to Niamh but really said to everyone, 'What is the big deal about the playground? Why do they want to go there so bad?'

'It's a mystery,' Niamh replied, her voice singsong. The girls laughed very hard.

Apparently oblivious to this, Studzy said to John, 'Come on, move.'

The problem here, of course, was John could not move. He could not let them see him in full, fully, and he sought to suggest this tender predicament to his pal with a candid shake of the head, a slight manoeuvre away from the steps. His friend must know his trouble, there must be an appreciation drawn from dressing rooms, where John would never remove his T-shirt before shrugging on the goalkeeper's jersey, from John's pitiful quietness whenever the word 'fat' was uttered even generally in school, from the incident with Snorlax. 'What you waiting for?' Studzy said. There was no emotion in his face. Visible contempt would have at least allowed John to reciprocate the anger, repackage it and call Studzy a name, ask him what *he* was waiting for. 'One second, like,' John said. How could his friend not understand? Probably the girls were thinking: Why won't the fat boy get out? The girls were thinking: Everyone can see he is a fatso so what is the problem? Studzy said, 'Will you move,' and John mumbled incoherently and there was pressure behind his eyes – he was a public crier, and his mam had explained once this was a virtuous attribute, but not right now, not right here – and then as if shattering through glass with each stroke forward, the girls shifted by the boys – Karen passing John an odd smile – and swiftly departed up the steps.

Niamh's face strayed over her shoulder. Karen's did not bother. Both their one-pieces were navy and clung to them in the special areas like wound clingfilm. And from their slender shoulders, liquid glistened on and off like tiny mirrors and tiny earrings as they vanished down the open archway.

'What's wrong with you?' Studzy said to John, but low now, private.

John teetered by the hotel's brown and green and rubbish bins. Studzy was beside him, directing a snake on his phone, one foot periodically itching the other. The girls had not come out yet. There was the rancid gag of waste and mushying food. The sun was still bright, and the heat mingled in this stink, stewed it so it coiled up furry in John's nostrils. The boys had not spoken in the changing rooms and, once outside, Studzy had only said, 'This is it,' followed by, 'You better cop on.' John was dressed in baggy jeans and a baggy jumper imprinted with a tidal wave. Studzy wore a black WuTang hoodie and trackies. The boy's gear was bundled up in two towels at their feet. John wasn't sure specifically why he had to cop on, but he did not doubt for a second its underlying truth.

Five minutes now waiting and there was this increasingly unlikeable silence that wasn't silence – Studzy growled criticisms at himself, a car pulled in and out of the car park, the phone beeped soullessly – and so John decided he should be thirsty. He hunched towards Studzy. 'Actually. Can we go Cotter's? I need a Coke, or something.'

Studzy did not look up. 'Didn't you hear me?' He tssked at his phone and stashed it in his pocket. A zipping sound and Studzy said, 'We have to go straight to the playground. That's where it will happen, right?' He checked behind him as if the bins might be bugged. 'There is this wall. My brother told me about it. Him and the lads use it for their girls.' Studzy began to rub his thumb and middle finger together to indicate – what? Fire? Money? Kissing? Fingering!? John could not comprehend the cryptic gesture and yet brainlessly it clicked deep within him, like bad news read on another's face. He needn't understand what it meant, only what it implied. And what it implied was sordid and amorous and inappropriate and wasn't that what he sought to reap from today?

'I was thinking that, too.' John dragged a heel along the curb. 'Yeah, no,' he said, 'I thought the playground be smart, like.'

Studzy nodded. His expression was set to severe and cross – contours at his brows, thin chalky lips, a subtle morphing of his scar to a Nike tick – and then this relaxed, evaporated as Studzy asked, 'Did you do that religion yoke? For the confirmation book. You know, what you're grateful for.'

Obviously, John had. He was grateful for his Nana, and his Fabien Barthez goalkeeping gloves, and that vast landscape encompassed by Sports.

'Can I copy it?'

Before John could agree, though with rigorous stipulations which he'd hope would ultimately deter Studzy from copying, they heard the bristled purr and slam of the aluminium doors. Unthinkingly, the boys stepped from one another. The girls sauntered out with bags – pink and zebra – on their backs, both straps surprisingly in use. Their hair was long now, and seaweed-like between the kink of their shoulders and neckline. In random streaks, Niamh's hair was crisper in colour. Russet. A want to yank this hair and sniff it creeped through John and he averted his eyes.

'Heya,' Karen said.

The boys probably should have returned a hello, an unbright hey, but Studzy skipped over this for them and went through to teasing the girls, 'Take you that long to do your makeup?'

Niamh took a swig from a Lucozade Sport bottle. She lowered it almost immediately. The bottle let out a soft sucking noise. 'Yuck,' she said. 'What's that smell?' She had a clip in her hair. It was a butterfly.

'Ha Ha, Enda,' Karen said.

Studzy enjoyed this. He elbowed John.

'From the bins,' John said to Niamh. 'It's from the bins.' John tilted sideways so she might more clearly see the bins.

Niamh pulled a face. Her lips were dewy, and John also noted, when she next spoke, they were tinted a weak pink. A fluffy dressing-gown pink. 'Are you guys ready?' she asked.

They struck left from the hotel. Girls first, boys second. The playground was adjacent to the sprawling beach at the very end of Keel. The road dipped and as they went, John inhaled the girl's moist, sugary scent and found himself intently studying their gait. Their walk amazed him in the way things didn't anymore, in the way dinosaurs used to. How they stepped with such grace and ease, how they strode as if they were atop an inch or two of woolly air, and, yet, his own boxy feet, in comparison, did *this* over and over again, did it clumpy and wrong over and over again.

John tried to slow his steps, pace them to match theirs. Then he tripped on a rifted edge of slab, bounced forward.

Studzy stared.

John pretended the bounce was normal. He bounced once more for effect.

It was April. They looped down another road, wider, a steeper descent.

Soon they passed the post office and the bankvan, hitched up but padlocked, and a fluorescent Centra, where the automatic doors opened as they bounded by. The wafting smell from the deli of spicy chicken and potato wedges, like that of over-worn socks and heaped runners by the back door. Swinging around on her tippy-toes, Karen asked Studzy if his brother was still mad for Niamh's sister, still texting and calling her twenty-four-seven. John saw Niamh glance up at Karen. A scoff and Studzy answered, No way. What you on about? Sure, his brother had a girlfriend. Karen just smiled. There again, dimples.

They were around the corner and down the next street when an old dear poked out from an oaken doorway across the road. She was smoking and her jaw protruded like a pulled drawer. Studzy said, 'Take a watch at this feek.' He bopped his hips forward and back, spanked an imaginary chest-tall something or other. This was the act of sex, and John laughed. Except John was a little sad staring over. He had seen his mam chat to this old dear before, handing her boxes, envelopes, inviting her for dinner, but she also looked funny and so, John understood, it was her own fault.

'State of her,' John said, biting his cheek.

The girls were too far ahead to hear them.

'Imagine shifting her,' Studzy said, and his mouth was open. He had upped the stakes.

John laughed and absently tugged at his fly. There was a wanton thrill even in this grim dreaming. 'Imagine, like? Be so rotten,' John said in a lowered voice. The girls were still way ahead, and John spurred himself to go further, to beat his friend, 'Fucking her, like. Can you picture that?' The first time he had used such a combination of words. A salted aftertaste. Now Studzy was hoarse with laughter, convalescing with laughter. Swabs of saliva around his teeth and John spat at the ground. 'Just fucking it in and out of her.' Never mind that fucking evoked only a dictionary definition in his head, never mind that at all. 'The manky bitch,' John said with genuine disgust.

The girls had started walking back towards the boys, cautiously.

Still giggling, Studzy handed his towel to John and John said, 'Do it,' without knowing what his friend was about to do. Studzy's face clenched and then he tromped across the road.

'Hello, hey,' Studzy said. He was inching towards the old dear, and his voice went squeakier as he pointed at John and asked, 'Will you suck my friend's willy?'

Hysterics at this. It was funny. It was too far and it was funny.

The old dear squinted at Studzy. 'What?' she said, and, recoiling, she flapped away smoke.

Niamh and Karen flanked John, and Niamh offered him a weak smile.

Karen shouted, 'What are you doing, Enda?'

Studzy looked back. A crowd, an audience.

Could John have roared at Studzy to stop there, that it was gas enough already? Could he have ushered Studzy harmlessly away from the old dear? Could John have done anything other than watch and hiccup with glee once Studzy flicked the cigarette from her gob, once Studzy brought his middle fingers right to her stunned face? Probably, but it did not feel like that at the time. It did not feel like John could do anything but howl and cheer. The three of them immediately hurtling after the already bolted Studzy, screaming though they themselves had done nothing wrong. As John sprinted, his gaze was fisheyed and there were brash, highlighter colours surrounding, but there was no definition of buildings or faces. The only solid was their shared laughter, the only solid texture he could make out was their laughter foaming above and now behind as they bombed down the blurred street. A chant of you little bastards. You little cunts. And something was flung at them. Turning, John saw it. An ashtray split cleanly in two. Royal blue. The ash scattered across the path, a puff of it hovering from their rush. Choking with jubilation, his legs were pounding and pounding, and the girls were alongside him. The clacking of whatever was inside their schoolbags. The old dear whisked a cane aloft and this was also thrown, and John watched in slow motion her bulk stumble and collapse backward. They laughed harder, ran harder, and caught up with Studzy, who cried: Did you see that? In the distance, the flash and smear of sea and, before it, the humped metal belonging to the playground.

Honestly, Studzy had barked in John's ear, she likes you. Karen told me, so. How exciting was this knowledge, how disorientating and bonkers it was as a concept to behold. Niamh, a girl, liking him. How it sent an electric current hammering through his entire body. Someone liked you. John thought: I wish this wasn't happening and this is everything I ever wanted. You just have to come with me, Studzy had insisted. And she'll shift you. I'm nearly positive she will. However unlikely and improbable it was, John wanted to believe his friend.

An uncomfortable thumping from within and John was bent over with hands on his knees. The sensation of blood spurting from his ears and he inspected and, thankfully, there was no scarlet on his hand. He was huffing open-mouthed to try to ease the fire in his lungs, and it was like a bike pump, the haggard din being released. Haw, haw, haw. 'Wow,' Studzy gasped, 'Wow-wee.' Studzy was on his haunches and he rose now, clapping. 'No way that happened.' The girls were ruddy cheeked, and they sort of hugged. On Niamh's forehead, a lock of hair was glued vertically. A lightning crack. It wasn't brown or russet: this hair was oddly bronze. 'She fell,' John managed, and frenzied agreement was echoed: Yeah, yeah, yeah, the old dear had fallen. They were in the playground. Tumbling waves as background music. Sweat dwindled under his arm and it beaded his upper lip and John didn't care. Why should he now? Look where he was, who he was with. It was magical. Straightening, he was momentarily woozy, oily dots and globes and UFOs rippling through his sight, and then they washed off and John was only happy.

'Oh my god,' Karen brayed. 'Enda. How could you?'

Studzy put his hands to his chest. 'What did I do?'

Everyone laughed.

'I can't believe it,' Karen said, repeated this. Sand was strewn all over the rubber flooring of the playground, glittering. John brushed his jumper down and brushed it again.

'That was crazy.' Niamh searched each of their faces, a circuit for her own disbelief. Her eyes were wide, and her fingers rested on either rosy cheek; waxy indentions where they pressed upon skin, and her wrists met below, so it was like a gaping tulip. John saw her pretty face as a tulip. 'Enda, did you know her?' Studzy shrugged and she turned the question to Karen and John, 'Did you guys know her?'

John said he had never seen that old woman before. She was nuts though. Wasn't she? Wasn't she batshit? Karen's reply was rapid and unintelligible to John, but it was eagerly received by Niamh, who pared the bronze from her forehead. When John looked up again, the girls were ambling towards the swings, almost tripping into one another.

All of a sudden, John recalled the point of the day and it seized him to search for it.

And there it was.

Off to the side of the playground, over a verging ditch and a defeated barrel of copper wire. An unconnected, unfinished wall in a field skinned with brackish soil and stalks of hay. Just there stranded in the field in the way the turf stack was just there in the garden. It was not hidden; it did not seem romantic. Ratty takeaway bags and cans bloomed at its base. John thought of a thumb rubbing a middle finger.

Studzy said to the girls, 'The swings. Seriously. Are ye babies or what?' No reaction, but John loudly concurred. 'Yeah,' John said, 'Two babies.' Studzy looked at him and wandered in the direction of the climbing wall but seemed to reconsider halfway and went instead to the slide opposite the swings. There, he stiffened by the ladder, and John noted a confidential incline of chin, a signal John recognised from school, from hints to follow and top your pencil at the bin.

John broke towards him.

They posed with their backs to the girls, their eyes stuck on the foot-grooved steps of the slide. Rightaway, John was unable not to ask was that the wall Studzy's brother was on about? To which Studzy responded in monotone: What do you think? John folded his arms, but did not like what this gave his chest, so unfolded them. The buttery popcorn smell of his and Studzy's collected sweat. The complaining mew of the swings as they rocked. John looked over at the girls, how they chatted, conspired, and he glanced at the wall, and though he predicted more slagging, he wondered out loud, 'What happens at the wall?' Studzy smoothed a hand through his clipped hair and sought to groom what little could be groomed. John continued, his voice climbing, 'Like. What do I do there?'

'I shouldn't have done that to your one,' Studzy said then. He shook his head, blinked like something was in his eye. 'I really shouldn't have done that.'

Under his breath, Studzy cursed at himself. He started to say mean things about himself.

Studzy was correct: he shouldn't have done it, and yet he had. And that decision was precisely why they were pals, John thought. It was why John liked him despite not really liking a whole lot about him. Because John would never in a thousand years do such a horrible thing, but Studzy would do such a horrible thing every day if he was so disposed, or so shoved. It was an unforeseen confession, yes, but John found he was warmed by it all the more. The pleasant glow of a friend's mistake and moral failure. John would like to see him punished now. For Guards and sirens. For Studzy's dad to be summoned with a fiery poker. 'Probably not,' John answered then, with a smack of his lips to imply judicial deliberation. 'Yeah, you really shouldn't have done that,' he added cruelly. 'Very bad by you.'

Studzy winced and began to chew at his thumbnail, like a rat against horsehair rope.

John waited and waited and then said, 'It was gas though. And I think the girls loved it.'

'Really?' Studzy said.

John swore, and Studzy inhaled and thanked him.

From the swings, Karen said, 'You guys want to head to the shop? Or do something else?'

Niamh was shaking her head.

'Hold on,' Studzy shouted without turning around. His foot was jouncing against the ground. An arm – his left – was now flexed inward toward his collarbone so that it seemed lame. It was getting chilly. The wind was growing.

'Will you ask Niamh to shift me?' Studzy said, and it felt like when a ball unexpectedly skips over John's swinging foot, the loss of ruling gravity and the embarrassment and the slowness of what in reality must be incredibly fast. John looked directly at him. He looked directly at Studzy to confirm he was being serious here, he looked at his friend in the hope that his eyes or lips or that paled scar would change what had been asked into a misunderstanding. But they did not. 'Will you?' Studzy said in a raised whisper.

John replied, 'I will, yeah.' He reiterated this confirmation twice and kept talking without meaning to. 'You know if Niamh liked me before, then she is bound to like you? I know she will.' He meant this and it felt important to him to emphasise it. 'She'll definitely like you if she liked me. Hundred percent, she will.'

'That was all made up,' Studzy said. 'She never liked you.' There was no change in his voice. 'It was a joke. You didn't believe that, did you? She never liked you.' He looked sidelong at John. 'We all made that up. It was a joke.'

'Oh, I know that,' John answered. 'No. I knew that.' Did his voice crack? Did it waver? 'I thought it was funny,' he went on. 'I'm just saying.' What was he saying? His fingers nipped at his jumper so that it didn't stick to his stomach. John said, 'I knew it was a joke.'

It occurred to John that he was almost being truthful here: from the beginning, the deepest pit of him had probably recognised it as a joke. Of course, it was a joke. Of course it was. How could she possibly like him? And it was a funny joke, so what harm? John had known all along – kind of – so what harm? You only mock the people you really like, so what harm? The sun was bright, still bright, and the lapping sea wasn't blue at all, and, pining for a distraction, John gaped at the grassy dunes over by the small metal gate of the playground. His head swam. The grass curled and swished like joint writing, then it stilled and the green faded and John looked up at cloud where the sun had been. 'I'll ask her for you. I'll do it now,' John said to Studzy. He didn't have to force this. These words came out easy. 'No problem.'

And it was no problem. Without delay, John walked across with hands tucked in pockets, and he said his line, 'Will you shift my friend?', and Niamh's mouth opened partly and she faced Karen and her see-through braces glinted like sugar and Karen stared past John and he waited for Niamh to turn back but she didn't and there was a disarming umm noise before Niamh said, defensively, 'No.' And when John had nothing to argue to this, she said, 'I'm sorry.'

John said, 'Ah, right.'

In the afterwards, there was no opportunity for John to tenderly inform Studzy of his rejection, maybe spice his explanation with a lie involving Niamh's braces, for as soon as John spun round, Karen jumped off the swing and pushed by him. She was pursued by Niamh. A rattle as their seats crashed and the ringed chains mangled together. Wordlessly, the girls began to gather their bags in the centre of the playground. Studzy's answer was plainly before him. Were they all leaving now? John watched Studzy for movement, a guiding sign, but there was none. Studzy only reached for his phone. 'We're going for food,' Karen eventually explained, bucking a shoulder to reposition her bag. Her voice had tightened, and she looked only at Studzy. Niamh's arms were wrapped around her. She didn't look at anyone. 'Alright,' Studzy said, his thumb pounding the phone. 'Bye, so.' He slumped against the slide's steps, his demeanour wildly suggesting this was in fact a very comfortable stance. But his face was red like they had only just raced, and it betrayed everything.

Having first freed the entwined swings, John went to join Studzy at the slide. They surveyed the girls' hike back up Keel until their figures turned right on the main street and disappeared from view. Or at least it seemed like they did this together. How could John be sure? Then John muttered about training tomorrow, and the lift, as if they had not discussed it, and he mentioned the old dear who had fallen and how that was gas, and it was just himself talking and talking so he stopped. The girls had not latched the gate after them, and it swung back and forth. A thunking then a clicking sound like a turnstile. He heard that and the building whoosh of the sea and Studzy's breathing. John had not bothered to grant consolations about Niamh, nor did he provide Studzy with generous falsehoods to whittle down her rejection into a cosy maybe. His silence and the lack of firm clarification likely made it far sorer for his friend. John kind of hoped so, anyway.

To speak, John asked for the time.

Studzy was texting, and when he put the phone away, he picked at his ear with his baby finger. Then he pouted at this finger. 'I didn't want to shift her. I thought she wanted to shift me,' he said. 'That's the only reason I got you to ask.'

The boys exchanged a look.

'Yeah. It's gone four,' Studzy said, and he rubbed his palms on the thighs of his trackies as if they were mucky. 'By the way, I can ask Karen if she'll shift you, if you want?'

Clearly he would not actually do this. Karen and Niamh will never be brought up again in John's company, John felt sure of that. But it was a nice offer regardless. Or at least it was an offer, however disingenuous. It was a kind of kindness and John was not at all fussy.

'I might get you to do that, actually,' John said. 'Maybe, yeah.'

'Sound,' Studzy said. 'I'm not sure she'll get with you, like, but I can ask.'

'Yeah,' John said, 'that's fine.'

The thought struck and John said, 'I mean. Ye*aaa*h.'

There was no sharky grin at this. No rewarding giggles. Studzy retrieved his phone again and groaned as the screen lit up. 'I better head.' He held out the phone. 'Dad's onto me.'

Though it was too early for his own lift home, John replied, 'Same.'

And what happens next in the story? Is the boys' friendship doomed from here? Will they soon split apart? Will they become mortal enemies? Will they be the kind of fellas who will hold a petty grudge for the rest of their lives? What do you think?

Or maybe they will stay friends, buds, and the resentment between them will shimmer below the surface, ticking beneath until it will all explode over a minor and insignificant act at the Debs, and they will come to blows, their dates screaming at them to stop, and they will leave one another bloody-mouthed and beaten? That could be next, actually. There is an ending.

Or possibly after this failed afternoon, they become estranged, not really friends and not necessarily enemies, just two boys that grow up in the same hole, that might not wish to knock shoulders at a house party but also do not wish to knock each other's teeth out? Is that it?

Perhaps this afternoon doesn't dent or change their relationship remotely – because why should it? What is so consequential about this afternoon, really? – and then what if the boy named John suddenly moves to Galway when he is properly thirteen, and as a result it's not as if the friendship formally ends – the boys would talk if they met, however unlikely, and they would be friends on social media, for sure – rather instead it runs aground because there are no shared waters anymore. And maybe these two friends live their respective lives as best they can and perhaps John remembers this afternoon and feels righteous animosity, or, possibly, John only recalls that time with sweetening nostalgia: when he was an innocent buck chasing girls alongside his friend.

And maybe the other boy eventually has a kid and he posts about them on social media, and John, being nosey, stumbles upon this photo one day – in the photo, the scar is a little more faded on his old friend's cheek but still there, still recognisable, almost touchable through the blue glow of the laptop – and though he doesn't click the like button below the photo – they have transferred to a new social network and they have not added each other as friends this time because they were friends years and years ago and they haven't interacted in years and years, so why should they? – the photo makes John smile. It makes John happy and full and yes, it also makes him remember what his old friend said to him once, the joke – because everything has to revolve around John eventually, everything has to be captured by his particular lens – but alongside this he remembers going bowling for a birthday and their slanted language and both nervously playing football with the older lads and then he no longer remembers anything between them because his family moved away and both boys grew up, lived on. Is that what happens next? Does it end with one boy smiling at an image of the other cuddling his baby years down the line? That would be pleasant. Can we drop the full-stop there? Can we say 'The End'?

Or does it move past that photo? Does it end when John hears randomly that his old friend, who held his child so proudly, so smiley, has hanged himself in a shed in some back garden? And after stumbling upon this news online,

John then hears it confirmed over the phone from his mother – you remember Enda, don't you? – and for the rest of the day John sorts through I-can't-believe-it-comments and clicks on profiles of people he once knew and he feels nothing but sick and he throws up and he cannot stop imagining the shed and he cannot push away the fact that he once contemplated the same lonely consequence, the same ending, and he thinks of his old friend and his sharky smile and that scar and he is hanging there and it is awful, more awful than anything John can say or think or write, and he can't reach out and he can't talk and he can't share and he doesn't drive down to the funeral because he doesn't know this man, because John knew the boy, and there was a difference between the two, he tells himself to feel better, there is a big difference between the two. And when John pictures the shed, it is exactly like the one in his own parent's back garden. And when he pictures his friend, lifeless, inside it, he doesn't see the young man he is, but the twelve-year-old he was. The twelve-year-old who John loved and feared. His friend. Is that what happens next? Is that our ending? Does the story have to end like this?

# ACKNOWLEDGEMENTS

Firstly, thank you to Ciara for her endless support, humour, patience and love. Thank you to Sally Rooney for casting her supreme eye all over these stories and offering the wisest advice, and for her warm friendship outside of these stories. Thank you to Tom Morris for his guidance and encouragement and random phone calls. I have been lucky to be able to send my work at every stage to Nicole Flattery and Michael Nolan, two brilliant writers and friends. Thank you to Niall MacMonagle for his kindness and enthusiasm. Thank you to Brendan and Mary for allowing me to house-sit. Thanks to the editors who published versions of these stories in *The Tangerine*, *Winter Papers*, *Granta*, *Banshee* and *The Stinging Fly*. While writing this book, I have been helped and encouraged by so many friends and writers. Thank you to: the BBB, Joe Joyce, Brian Gaffney, Ruth Storan, Sarah Moloney, Joe Crotty, Evan Jones, Rory Gleeson, Ferdia Lennon, Jacqueline Landey, Lily Meyer, Nick Padamsee, Nick Shadowen, Colin Barrett, Danny Denton, Maggie Armstrong.

Thanks to Mr Séamus Kelly of Coláiste Éinde for making me want to write. Thanks to John Kenny, Mike McCormack and Trish Holmes for teaching me how to write. Thanks to my classmates at UEA, and Andrew Cowan, Henry Sutton and Jean McNeil. Thanks to James Ryan and Éilís Ní Dhuibhne. Thank you to Gordon Snell and UCD for awarding me the Maeve Binchy Travel Award which helped shape some of these stories. I was also fortunate enough to receive two bursaries from the Arts Council of Ireland during the writing of this book, and I'm immensely thankful for this generosity.

Thanks to my agent Lucy Luck: I'm grateful for her unwavering trust in the short story. I'm grateful too for Aoife K. Walsh and her clarity, snappy efficiency and belief. Thanks to Neil Burkey, Stephen Reid and everyone else at New Island Books and beyond who has helped with the making of this book.

Thank you to my family: Nana and Granny, the parents, the Sister, the cousins, the uncles and aunts, the Brother-In-Law, the nephews, the two dogs, the white cat named Wilson. Finally, thank you to the Masterson sisters for their love, for their cackles, for the stories.